How I Got My Kicks on Route 66

Books by Ronn Perea

How I Got My Kicks on Route 66
(a.k.a. Smiles Giggles and Laughs)

Elsie and Elsa
Email Tango

How I Got My Kicks on Route 66

Ronn Perea

SPEAKING VOLUMES, LLC
NAPLES, FLORIDA
2022

How I Got My Kicks on Route 66
(a.k.a. Smiles Giggles and Laughs)

ISBN 978-1-64540-474-3

To the only ones that matter.

To Julian and Elsie Rose Perea, my Pop and Mom.

They were the only ones on planet Earth that could have put up with their crazy, wise ass kid. This was doing something that had never been done before with so much confidence.

And yes, they were very happy with the results.

Acknowledgments

The ladies that molded this work have my extreme gratitude for relieving me of my crossed eyes that they took on with a breeze: My Editors extraordinaire are Nicole Steele B., Royal Jones, Katie Grant, and Darlene S.

Prologue

The police car sped toward us, lights flashing as it careened past.

"Must have criminals to catch," I observed, pressing on the gas, taking myself, and the woman I proposed to tonight, away from an evening at my DUKE CITY COMEDY CLUB.

"Got a new tape, darling. It's another rendition of Route 66, done in high tech by Depeche Mode. Want to hear it?"

She helps pull the tape from the glove box. I tap the break when another red light flashes up ahead. She slides the cassette into the dashboard player.

Quadraphonic sound fills the car. The right front speaker emits the sound of a hubcap falling off. As we roll down the road, the sound of the hubcap spinning moves to the left front speaker. Still spinning, the hubcap stops on the street from the rear speaker. Behind me, heavy metal vocals come in on cue. "If you ever plan to motor west," they croon, "there is a byway, a highway to motor west. Get your kicks on Route Sixty-Six."

The lane in front of my Zephyr opens up, but I brake as we approach the light. The palm of Heather's hand rests on my thigh.

As I turn to her, she smiles up at me, and I again marvel at her beauty. I've done all right for myself. From the corner of my eye, I see the light up front turn green. I release the brake and we coast into the intersection—just as Heather shrieks!! I glimpse headlights approaching from my left. We're going to be hit!

"Oh, Ronnie!" A vehicle slams into my side of the car just above the front wheel well. The windshield shatters, showering us with a mist of particles. I can't seem to move.

Heather is still screaming, "No-oooo-oooo . . ."

We are slammed into a sideways slide. We suddenly move faster than before. The world spins around us like that hubcap from the speaker as Heather's cry goes on and on.

My seat belt isn't fastened, yet I am able to center myself in the bucket of the seat. Amazingly, I stay in place. Heather's seat belt holds her tightly, but I stretch out my arm in a useless attempt to protect her.

At that moment, as if in slow motion, her side of the car wraps around a steel light post. The Zephyr jolts to a stop astride the curb. The passenger side windows burst, spraying more glass. Metal crunches and my Mercury Zephyr sounds like a tin can being crushed. Heather ceases to scream.

It's only been a moment, but it's so quiet. Has the world stopped?

Steam hisses from the hood. Reality slowly returns to me. The stereo is still playing Depeche Mode's Route 66 when the flying hubcap spins to a stop once more.

Oh, how I wish I could start this night over . . .

Chapter One

The New Chinatown Restaurant's red neon marquee sign looms thirty feet over old Route 66, now called Central Avenue. The reader board proudly displays the club's main attraction, THE DUKE CITY COMEDY CLUB *Every Thurs *Fri *Sat Night. Through my camera lens, I adjust the sign until it's in focus. This is my fifth marquee photo of the day. These marquee photos from my mini comedy showroom circuit located in the hotel, the rock and roll nightclub, the steakhouse, and the theater will bring back memories, especially when I show them to my future kids as they sit on my lap.

But first, tonight has yet to come and my schedule is a big one and not typical either. I walk through the Chinese pagoda garden entrance. Trickling ponds and waterfalls that line each side of the walkway transform the arid desert climate to lush and humid; very inviting. It's with ease that I put the necessary large smile on my face. I must mentally prepare for this evening as I enter through the front swinging doors.

My mind is full. How should I handle tonight's five comics on stage? How about the important date I have with the prettiest young lady I've ever known (and I've known some), and how am I going to handle the interview appointment later with a radio station reporter?

It's a relief and a load off my mind that I don't have to be my usual Master of Ceremonies for tonight's show as I normally would. Fortunately, Lee Parks—The Continental Kid—is available to MC. As a magician, he gets steady work. As a smooth master of ceremonies, he is in high demand.

I frown every time I think about him. There is an uneasiness between us. And I know that it's simply an ego clash. On the other hand, I don't want to admit it, but we're aware of each other's talents. I know I'm a top-flight stage producer, organizer, public relations specialist, and creative businessman with enough ham personality characteristic to be the necessary front man. Lee is the most polished, top-flight professional magician/master of ceremonies in the entire state. Professionally, we need each other, but neither of us would admit it.

Customers mill about inside the busy Mandarin Chinese restaurant lobby. Among them are my DCCC All Stars and, of course, the restaurant owner, Harry Jew. With his Cheshire cat grin, he stands behind the green grotto area, his eye on the cash register, but it is his wife's sister, Katy, who is the real manager and master sergeant for the restaurant.

The story is that Harry inherited the restaurant from his father-in-law who started the Chinatown before World War II, making it one of the oldest restaurants in the state. Beautifully designed, its interior is filled with oriental statues and smiling Buddhas.

According to the national comedy club trade published out of Mill Valley, California, my comedy outfit is the only one located in a Chinese restaurant anywhere across America!

"You got many, many calls for your show tonight," Harry welcomes me.

My smile grows. "Of course, what do you expect?" I show my cocky grin. "With the strength of the lineup of comics we have for this weekend's shows, plus the full feature article in this morning's paper, how can we miss? Did you see it?"

Harry nods.

Because we all get paid off door receipts, I need a full house. As a result, I don't have the luxury of showing any normal insecurities about attendance levels. I must keep my fears locked up deep inside so, instead, I always smile. My motto is, "Always exude confidence!" It's a requirement for this job in the tower of power.

The phone rings behind the grotto. "It's probably another reservation," says Harry with a grin as he answers. "It's for you." He hands me the receiver.

"Hello? Hello? Baby?"

I recognize her voice right away. "Hi Heather!"

"When can you pick me up?" she asks with over excitement.

"I can't get away now. I just got here."

"Oh." She sounds so disappointed. "You mean we can't see each other tonight?"

That voice of hers always grabs at me.

"Darling, just call yourself a cab."

"Okay, I'm a cab," she jokes.

I smile. "Tonight I have a chance to do a radio interview. Then afterward you and I can enjoy some egg rolls and comedy."

"Oh baby, I can't wait to get there."

Her youth shows, and that is exactly what turns me on. At twenty-one, she's ten years my junior. "I'll see you soon," I tell her.

I know, I'm smiling. She makes me feel good. That's all that matters, and it's a great way to start the night. Now I might as well get into my usual show-night routine.

I walk through swinging doors into the rear of the kitchen. Meat cleaver in hand, a graying Chinese American man dressed in not-so-clean kitchen whites, shouts, "Joke man!" His cleaver continues chopping away at a table covered with fish. Another much younger Chinese man, the first assistant, chops at the red beef laid out on the next table. He smiles a welcome as well.

"We're going to have a busy night tonight, guys," I tell them.

The floor is wet and slippery as I approach the dish washing station. Two college age kids, twin brothers, are sweating while loading the never-ending stack of dirty dishes.

"Oh man, I wish we could see the comedy show," one says. The other one shoots in. "We always have too many dishes to wash during the show."

"Don't worry guys, you'll be able to catch the end tonight." I gesture for them to listen in. "Let me tell you something. My first job in show business was during high school, as a dishwasher in a supper club. Now I produce the show." I remember hating washing dishes, too.

Looking to the front of the kitchen and the food line of steam tables and hot lamps, I see the chef preparing his orders. Behind him, the grill is filled with sizzling meats. Next to it is the deep fryer. My eyes flicker at what I really came in here for. Next to the fryer sits a full pan of plump, steaming egg rolls. Glancing around to be sure no one can see me, I grab my lucky egg roll.

I make a quick exit through the swinging doors, I stand out of sight. In the middle of an idle wait station, my smile grows as I chew and munch down the fried and crispy, crackling egg roll.

Soon I lick my fingers clean as it's become time to enter the show-room.

There waiting is my master-of-ceremonies, Lee Parks. His class shows, dressed in a black tux, accented with a gold bow tie and matching handkerchief, he carries his slim 5'6" frame well. The magician holds onto his black traveler's trunk filled with his bag o'tricks. He must have had a haircut; his blond hair seems more closely cropped and his goatee is smartly trimmed.

"Who's on the lineup tonight?" he asks.

"I'll kick it off, then introduce you," I say. "Open with fifteen minutes. The marine, Bill Thomas, will do his five minutes, then you'll segue, of course. I want Silver up there next. She'll lead into Willy's act."

"Do you think it wise putting up those two back to back? Willy doesn't like following her, and you know that."

"Well, what would you do? I've only got Alpine Bob left and where would you put him with that act of his? He's as late night as you can get."

"No argument there. If you have to put up Alpine, I'll set up my gear."

By the tone of his voice and expression on his face, it is easy to tell that he's not happy to be on the same stage with Alpine Bob. The rectangular showroom is filled with large round tables of eights, fours and twos. The chairs all face the mural of a gold-draped Buddha on the wall behind the stage. It oversees the backs of all the performers. Many of the comics do say they feel someone watching over their shoulder on this stage.

A petite, black haired waitress, a beauty of Chinese heritage, approaches me.

"There is someone here asking for you," she snaps and quickly turns to walk away.

I shrug. Apparently, she is still upset with me, but if anyone should be upset, it should be me. A couple of months ago, I brought in a traveling playboy type comic from Los Angeles. Buzz Alto was his name. Those two spent some time together. Then Buzz went back home after the usual week's gig without giving her his number. The next thing I know, the woman's mad at me for bringing this guy into her life. She asked me for Buzz's number, but I had to refuse. It is a cardinal sin to give out performers' phone numbers.

If she had initially explained that her doctor had required it, I would have complied immediately. Apparently, Buzz left her with a gift of a venereal nature and had no way to contact him. But no, instead she got the health department to send me a court order, requiring compliance.

Only then did I learn the details. I have to shake my head. Even though I had nothing to do with their incident, I caught all the flack and had none of the pleasure. As the producer, all I can do is shrug it off because it goes with the job.

A tall, balding man walks into the lobby and reaches out to shake my hand. "How are you, guy?" He holds a cassette tape recorder. "Bill Peterson, KKOX FM news. Thank you for seeing me."

"Are you kidding?" Smiling, I shake his hand. "I'm the one who's happy you were able to come."

I remember how I've been working on this radio station for months with weekly press releases. It's about time this guy finally showed up.

Not waiting for the Maître d', I lead the radio reporter through the Oriental environment. All the glass-enclosed, private formal dining rooms are busy except for one. I snap it up.

"I hope you haven't eaten. The food here is top notch."

"Well, I have already eaten," Bill replies. Still he examines the menu.

"Egg rolls! You can't come to a Chinese restaurant and not order their egg rolls," I say.

An oriental waiter brings two glasses of water to the table. "Thaddeus, please bring us a round of your rice egg rolls with tea."

"Anything for the Godfather of Comedy," the waiter responds with a smile. "That was a nice article about you in this morning's paper," the waiter adds as he walks away.

"Godfather of Comedy?" inquires the reporter.

"Yeah. The Journal did a story in the morning's edition on our new form of entertainment in Albuquerque: The Comedy Club. They ran my photo with a caption calling me the Godfather of local comedy."

Bill acts unimpressed. "I'll have to pick up a copy." He places the tape recorder in the center of the table and presses the record button.

"So, Ronn. Comedy in a Chinese restaurant? Why?"

How many times have I been asked that question, I wonder? "Why not? We started downtown at the El Rey Theater where we were packing them in. Harry Jew came in one weekend at my request. I wanted to increase seating capacity and upscale my show's environment. Harry had this idle dining room up here and he liked the smiles, giggles and laughs we were making. Well, the rest is history."

"Where do you get all your comics?"

"It's as crazy as King George the Third! The word got out that stand-up comedy was being performed downtown. Aspiring funny people seemed to come out of the woodwork and from all walks of life. They all fancied themselves comics. The next thing you know, we're putting ten plus funny bone artists on stage a night. Then a month ago, I produced a live radio comedy show on the university's radio station. That got the word out further. The next thing we knew, we had even more people who wanted to go on stage than we had time for in a night."

"You have that many good comics?" Bill asks.

"I didn't say that. About half show promise, others are diamonds that need polishing, and some, well, some I simply don't encourage."

"You mean, you tell people they're no good?" Bill looks shocked.

"Of course not. I don't need to. If the audience doesn't laugh, they learn quickly enough. If they want to, I'll let them on stage another time but in an open mic environment. Sooner or later they'll either get better or get discouraged. Believe it or not, it takes care of itself."

Thaddeus brings two steamboats to the table. Bill's eyes widen as the waiter uncovers several plump egg rolls.

"Thanks Thaddeus."

"Anything for the Godfather."

The waiter leaves the table with a teasing smile on his face.

I gesture toward the food. "Taste these. They're great. I never liked egg rolls till I started doing comedy here, now I'm addicted. They're on me."

Wasting no time, the reporter chomps a roll down in four bites, washing it down with a sip from the tiny teacup. Immediately, he starts on his second.

"So, with things going well for you, how do you feel about that new comedy club opening?" he asks with a full mouth.

My stomach plummets. This is the first time I've heard about any new comedy club. Struggling to keep my composure, I don't know how to answer him. I just pick up an egg roll.

Fortunately, a hesitant Thaddeus approaches. "Ronn, your comics are arriving and one of them is . . . well . . . asking for you."

I jump at the chance to sidestep the question. "Bill, finish here and enjoy. I've got to get things ready to go. The show starts shortly." I shake his hand. "I've got a table reserved for you in the front row, center."

The radio reporter appears impressed with front row center seats. Little does he suspect what he is in for. Front row center means he will be easy pickings for all the comics all night. By the end of the evening, everyone in the audience will know who Bill Peterson, KKOX news reporter, is.

Chapter Two

As I walk back into the showroom, all the comics are gathered around the performers' table. The first ones seen are Mr. and Mrs. Cordova.

"Greetings William, oh excuse me, Weely. Hi, Irene! How'd it feel to have your name in black and white this morning?"

"They didn't quote Weely's lowrider jokes right," she replies. "I write his material. I know how they're supposed to read. And they didn't—" she says.

Weely grips her hand on the table. "Any press is good press, Ronn. Here . . . something for you."

He hands me a two-by-four foot sheet of aluminum. Confused, I look it over. Engraved in red ink is this morning's newspaper article complete with the photo.

"What is this? Is it for me?" I ask. Then I add, "This is great!"

"It's the template," says newspaper printer by day, Weely.

I'm touched. "Thank you, thank you. Nifty."

I show it around to the other talents with pride.

Silver Vega has to throw in her two cents. "Why didn't that reporter mention me in the article?"

I can only reply by simply saying, "Ask your own boyfriend who wrote the article," I smirk.

She huffs and puffs. "Well I have to go get ready."

As she walks away, all the men she passes snap their heads to view her as she wiggles by, and you can tell by her smile, she knows it too.

"Is Alpine Bob here yet?" I ask Lee.

"It's almost show time," he replies. "He's probably on another binge."

I shrug as my guts churn.

"I brought a friend who's a magician," Lee says. "I'd like to give him some stage time."

"You asking or telling?"

"He'll help the lineup."

Lee points toward a guy sitting alone on one side of the comics' table, dressed in tux, tails and handkerchief. Lee waves him over.

"Let me introduce you."

Jumping to attention with a smile, the man strides toward us.

"Hello," he says. "Paul Lott here, magician extraordinaire. How do you do, Mr. Greco?"

We shake and I feel a deformed hand in my grip.

"Fine and dandy." Twisted fingers fill my palm. "Please call me Ronn. So, you're a magician, huh? How long have you been performing?"

"I had an act in Vegas until a few years back when I had a motorcycle wreck. This would be my first time back on stage. I'd really appreciate the opportunity. I've been rehearsing every day," he says and softly repeats himself. "Every day."

"Tell you what, Paul. If our headliner doesn't show up, you can open."

I pull my MC aside. "What's the scoop on this guy?"

"He's recovering from a mean bike wreck that laid him up for years; has a metal plate in his skull. I haven't seen him perform since he crashed, but he was a top act on the casino circuit in Vegas. It's worth giving him a shot."

I glance back at Paul. "Well, give him five minutes—with or without Alpine Bob."

I motion to the ex-magician, "Yo! Pauly, welcome aboard. Prep up your best five minutes. You're first out of the gate.

"Lee, open with some stand-up just to make sure you guys don't do the same material." I then glance at my comics then my watch. "Showtime in ten! Get ready, you laugh-meisters."

Paul grins. "Thank you, Mr. Greco—uh, Ronn." He digs into his bag of tricks in preparation.

As the producer of this outfit, I need a few minutes myself to be alone to get primed, psyched, and energized for the show. It's my private time. With quick steps, I head toward my favorite spot outside the New Chinatown Restaurant to sit by the waterfall pouring into a pond. The sound relaxes me. With several deep breaths, I count back slowly from ten to one. I slap my face a couple of times to get the blood running as I stand.

Moments later, I'm standing behind the showroom's lighting control board. It's time. With another deep breath, I slide down the toggle light switches. The room goes dark, then silent. I flip the second toggle switch. Pretaped music plays through the speakers. Nat King Cole's rendition of "Route 66" up to the verse "Get Your Kicks on Route Sixty-Six." As rehearsed, Lee takes over the switchboard so I can walk onto the darkened stage. The music fades. The follow spotlight cuts a narrow light beam through the darkened room to focus directly on a single microphone on its stand at center stage.

I stand with my large smile behind the microphone. With a snap, I stretch my arms out wide.

"Friends, Duke City-ites, and comedy aficionados, lend me your ears! For we do not come here only to chomp egg rolls or cry in our beer, but to smile, giggle and laugh! HOW DO YOU DO?!"

My smile grows with the enthusiastic sound of hands slapping together.

"Greetings, folks! For those of you who do not know me, I am your humble . . ." in the back of my mind I think to myself, 'Humble, yeah, right,' "comedy club producer, Ronn Greco."

As the applause strengthens, I notice a twenty-something female in a pink dress sitting up front, squeezing her date's arm.

"Before we get started, I want to thank columnist Dave Steinberg for the nice review in this morning's paper about the Duke City Comedy Club and moi. Thank you!"

Applause reaches its peak.

"Enough about that," I add. "Folks, as your producer, I must say we have a topnotch show for you tonight! The Crème De La Crème of New Mexico funnybone artists will stand on this very spot, in front of you, baring their comic souls." As my conscious mind delivers this intro, I subconsciously make a decision about Alpine Bob. The S.O.B. isn't here yet. He won't be going on stage tonight, even if he shows up later.

"Headlining tonight's comedy extravaganza is a fellow some of you have seen and demanded I bring back for more! This is a pleasure. Your favorite lowrider comic and mine, the most eminent lowrider there is . . . William 'Weely' Cordova!"

Applause bursts out again. Surprised, Weely grins.

"Then, of course, we cannot forget that Saucy Señorita, Silver Vega!" A spattering of applause follows.

"Also, tonight, the comic pride of the United States Marine Corp., Corporal Bill Michaels!" The room rips open with whoops, hollers and thunderous applause from the table at the back filled with Bill's buddies and fellow marines.

"It appears Corporal Bill has brought out the marines," I add while stretching my hand out to the troop of Marines sitting in the middle of the room. "And now a warning . . . Prepare to keep your eyesight sharp. A certain practitioner of the mystical art of magic is here to amaze you.

Performing for the first time for us tonight, making a comeback performance since his days in Vegas, you will see, Paul Lott!"

I encourage audience applause with some of my own.

"But now, it's time to introduce your Master of Ceremonies. He's a Master Magician in his own right, how about a healthy round of applause for Lee Parks!"

Applause fills the room. I walk off as Lee walks on. We pass and shake hands before he takes the mic. Enjoying the center stage's full attention, he extends his arms in front of him and rotates his wrists with a grand motion. All eyes focus on his closed fists.

We've done this routine many times before. Standing on my cue mark at the rear of the room near the light switches, I quickly shut off the follow spotlight. A microsecond of pitch-black darkness blinds everyone in the showroom. Lee's spot on stage is accentuated with a fire flash of golden orange sparkling flame.

I flip the spotlight switch again. Its beam of light captures the calm, cool and collected, impeccably dressed, now slyly smiling Parks.

"Good evening, Ladies and Gentlemen. My name is Lee Parks, and I am your MC this evening." As he bows, I flip another toggle switch and elevator music fills the room.

Snapping into action with sharp movements, Parks gracefully begins his act. In the background, music from a piano emphasizes his motions. Illusionist arms snap and stretch outward, revealing nothing up his long tuxedo sleeves. With precise movement, his right arm moves inward, his hand curling into a fist. Then, with his other hand, he points his index finger to lead the audience's eyes to his clenched fist.

Lee pokes his finger in, then out, revealing the tip of a white cloth. Continuing to pull, he produces a black cloth that leads to a red cloth tied to a blue cloth. Then a green cloth becomes visible, then a yellow cloth, and finally the white cloth again. The audience responds with building applause.

Taking a moment for myself, I stroll back into the lobby.

There, with his grand smile, stands Harry Jew.

"We're underway." I tell him as I lean on the counter of the grotto.

"Aren't you going to watch your own show?" he asks.

"How many times can any human watch the same show?"

Harry nods just as the glass front doors swing open.

Chapter Three

An apparently inebriated man wearing a tam hat staggers in with his arm around his latest groupie, Maggie. She started coming to his shows weeks ago and, after his act, she was all over him. Now, she's the longest running of Alpine's groupies. Her arm proudly circles his waist as if he were her trophy.

"Well, there's the big comedy producer man," rasps Alpine. "Your headliner has arrived!"

Several lobby patrons take notice. Some do a double take. Applause bleeds into the lobby from the showroom. Another round of applause signals Paul Lott's introduction.

My first impulse is to step back into the showroom to watch the new guy, but Alpine and his lady step into my space. Their body odor, a combination of sweat, stale liquor and cigar smoke arrives before they do. Alpine's eyes are the same as Maggie's, bloodshot. He staggers to attention while leaning into Maggie who tries to hold him steady.

"Don't you ever stop drinking?" I ask.

"Don't worry about it. I'm ready to go on," Alpine slurs.

"We've had this talk before. I don't want you drinking before you go on stage. You can't control it. Plus, have you seen the time? Have you? We started 15 minutes ago! You are canceled. Go cool your heels and drink some coffee or something." I have to turn my head just to take a breath. "Before I say anything I'll regret later, I'm going to go watch this new guy."

Leaving the sour-smelling couple behind, I walk back into my showroom. I'm in no mood for an argument from Bob or his groupie.

But things don't improve. As I walk into the showroom, I see that the audience is dead. Paul Lott is struggling with magic 101 cards, trying to do an illusion I've seen many times by countless aspiring trickologists who use this exercise for table magic, not for stage presentation.

"Card tricks? This guy is doing card tricks on my stage? Card tricks are for close up table magic," I comment to myself. No wonder the audience is bored!

Lee sits at the comics' table with chagrin on his face. Paul Lott has to get off—now. Anticipating what I am going to say, Lee whispers, "Give him the light?"

I nod. The comedy club's version of the old vaudeville stage hook is the flashlight. Lee shines it directly on his friend's face. All over the country, comics know that if you get the light, you have 60 seconds to wrap up your act and get off stage. No ifs, ands or buts. Everyone at the comics' table feels the struggling magician's pain but agree with the need for The Light. After all, it's happened to each of them at one time or another. I watch how Mr. Lott responds. The point is not to let the audience suspect he has been told to get off and Paul Lott shows professionalism by immediately and smoothly fading out of his act, then taking a bow.

Polite applause comes from here and there, the heartiest from his peers at the comics' table. As soon as Lott exits the stage, Parks replaces him.

"Give him a round of applause. Now, Ladies and Gents, let's keep it going!" He waits a beat. "May I introduce one of those very few in America today? A proud U.S. Marine stand-up comic. Put your hands together for Corporal Bill Michaels."

Lee exits stage left. Bill enters stage right causing the room to erupt with marine grunts.

Lee stands next to me. "Is Alpine Bob Volcano here yet? Not that it matters."

I nod. "He's drunk. Again."

Lee's face flushes red and veins pop out his temples. "I knew it! I knew it! You're not going to let him on, are you?"

Laughter fills the room. The Corporal gets in a couple of lines I don't hear. Lee gestures toward the lobby and I follow him out of the room. "Seriously. You're not going to put him on stage, are you?"

"Nope, but you know him."

"So? Come on, man. Don't you remember the last time? Your memory isn't that short, is it? You gotta do what's good for the show. He's blown it with everyone in the club. Why do you still put up with him?"

The first time Alpine went on stage under the influence, we all were learning about each other's personalities back then. In our young business relationship, it didn't dawn on me that rules like "No drinking before a performance" would be necessary. One night, Bob went on stage after more than a few shots of bourbon.

I remember those moments last year oh so well.

Chapter Four

One year prior

Lee Parks reenters the stage to present his next segue. He says nothing as he snaps out a wrist. He pulls down his sleeve to reveal nothing. With his other hand, he simply points to his naked wrist before snapping his fingers. To everyone's amazement, a fluttering pigeon appears in hand.

The audience claps in disbelief. He snaps his fingers again and another fluttering pigeon appears in his second hand.

The audience doubles the energy of their applause. Then Lee twists both wrists around each other causing both birds to disappear just as easily. The audience cannot help but stand to applaud. He absorbs his applause well.

"Thank you very much, ladies and gentlemen." He takes another bow. "Ladies and gentlemen, thank you. But now I would severely be remiss if I didn't announce the very special guest in our audience tonight. All in this showroom please give an Albuquerque welcoming to Country and Western national recording artist, CHARLIE PRIDE!"

He starts the audience applause himself as Charlie stands from his table filled with friends, before he takes a bow.

"Thank you, Mr. Pride." The applause subdues. "The time has come to introduce to you our next comic. Welcome, Alpine Bob."

He takes to the stage, like he always has, with his loud Bravado. At first, Alpine's act fills the room with laughs, but then it came.

"I understand we have a special group in the audience tonight. A group from the Native American Council is here." Alpine focuses attention toward a table in the back of the room. Six Native Americans of the Navajo Tribe sit enjoying the show. They are dressed in three-piece suits with empty cocktail glasses in front of them. They look embarrassed by the attention.

"Well, guys," Alpine starts . . . "I guess you know that I am from Missoula, Montana. We have Indians up there, too. We use them for the same reason you do down here, as insulation around the bars."

Tension fills the audience as nervous giggles sneak out. Without missing a beat, Alpine continued. "The other day I wanted to take in some Native American culture. I found a building with a sign out front that read Indian Cultural Center. I went in. It was a bar!"

This time the audience could not hold back. Laughter filled the room. The Navajos stirred angrily at their table.

Alpine went on. "Yeah, what do you call a white man who's surrounded by twenty Indians?" Not waiting for a response, he boomed, "A bartender!"

Laughter erupts.

Glassware crashes to the floor. "I don't like that, and I am not going to allow it to continue," shouts one of the best dressed Navajos. He stands up so fast he knocks his chair down. Cutting a path through the center of the showroom, he forces his way toward the stage.

The doorman reacted instinctively, intercepting the patron before he reached Alpine Bob. With professional smoothness, the man was ushered out calmly. His associates tumbled out with him.

Bob had impeccable timing and didn't miss a beat. "Well, Ladies and Gentlemen, I guess it's time for me to leave this stage. I have to go out to the parking lot and pull the arrows out of my station wagon! Good night!"

Appreciative applause guided him offstage as the audience thought it was all part of the show. No one suspected Alpine Bob was as buzzed as the angry patron.

But that wasn't the worst thing he did.

The next night was a slow Thursday at the Chinatown. Fortunately, only a few people were in the audience. How they got in, no one could ever explain, but a young couple was seated front row center with their three or four-year-old daughter. No sooner after Alpine started his act, he zeroed in on this young family.

Through liquor-clouded judgment, he stuck the microphone into the face of the little girl seated on her daddy's lap. What the setup to the joke was, no one cared. But what everyone heard were the words that are still burned forever in my mind.

"Hey little girl, ever seen your daddy jack off till his dick turned blue?"

Silence captured the showroom. It was so thick you could practically see it. With no questions asked, within a fraction of a second, Lee walked onto stage and grabbed the mic out of Alpine's hand who then stormed off.

A year later

He was banned from the club until only recently. Laughter from the showroom snapped me back to this present dilemma.

I confirm to Lee, "Weely will close the show."

He nods. Feeling a tap on my shoulder, I turn to see the bloodshot eyes of Alpine's groupie. I turn away.

"Can Bob talk to you?" she asks through beer breath.

With a reluctant sigh, I nod, and then frown at Lee. I follow Maggie to the lobby.

Alpine is leaning against the counter of the grotto. I dread even looking at him.

Before we can speak, a woman with a little girl crosses the lobby from the restroom. They pass by Alpine as he leans toward them. "Hey lady, how much you want for the little girl?" He laughs.

Shocked and appalled, the lady pulls the child closer before quickly stepping away, practically dragging the child with her.

Maggie laughs as well.

"What the hell is the matter with you?" I hiss at Alpine. "You're canceled tonight. Leave."

"You sonofabitch!" Bob blurts. "You said I could go up tonight."

I don't want to argue in the lobby. "If you want to talk to me, lower your voice."

Before his cash register only a few feet away, Harry Jew views everything before him. His demeanor changes for the first time in my memory as he explodes.

"How dare you come into my place and act like that? If you are going to argue, take it outside! Both of you, act like professionals." His Chinese accent comes out thick.

I am growing angrier by the moment. Because of this drunken, foul-mouthed, sonofabitch, my professionalism has just been justifiably challenged.

Through his stupor, Alpine responds as if physically threatened. "You want to fight. I'll fight," he slurs at me.

We exit through the front doors. Maggie follows close behind.

"You bastard. You're full of shit," Alpine accuses me as soon as we're clear of the building.

"Bobby, calm down. You shouldn't do this," Maggie pleads, grabbing his arm.

Bobby? I've never heard this garbage mouth called Bobby before.

"Listen to your girlfriend and calm down. Before you embarrass the comedy club again, go home before we both do something we'll regret."

"Embarrass?" Bob shouts. "Embarrass? You shit for brains. I have more talent than any of your so-called comics in there."

More patrons pass us going into the restaurant. Uncomfortable at being seen by the customers, I pull this colorful conversation out of sight by walking around to the side of the building. Bob follows, stumbling.

"I want to go on stage," he snaps. "I prepared a special act for tonight and I want to go on!"

"I told you to lower your damn voice when you talk to me." I continue to lead him further around the side of building.

"I'll talk any damn way I want. I'm a star comic."

"What a bloated ego. Listen, I have zero respect for you, Mr. Alpine Bob Bedard." It's been a while since I've been this formal with him. "No sir. I no longer require any of your services now or ever. I have to get back inside. This conversation is over. Goodbye." I turn to leave just as a yellow cab pulls into the parking lot. Damn. I completely forgot about my lady friend. I'll greet her as the cab pulls up.

Before I reach her, my shoulders are grabbed from behind. I spin around. Bob is livid.

"You bastard! You don't walk away from Alpine Bob! Are you going to put me on stage tonight?"

Jerking away, I finally raise my voice. "What did I just tell ya. Hell, no." Again, I turn away.

Again, Alpine grabs me, stopping me in my tracks. As he thrusts his face an inch from mine, he yells, "You lousy bastard! You are a sad excuse for a comedy producer, asshole, dick for brains."

His putrid body odor washes over me, and I can no longer stand it. My mind goes blank. With all my might, I throw a punch squarely into his face. To my surprise, Alpine staggers back but remains on his feet. For a nanosecond I feel shame at what little result there seems to be in my punch.

I guess Alpine must be liquor numbed. As if by a delayed reaction, he swings at me. I sidestep to the left, dodging the blow. Following through, and meeting zero resistance, Bob tumbles forward to the ground.

A shriek pierces the air. Maggie rushes over. "Oh, my God! Oh, my God!" Her high pitched, fingernails-across-a-chalkboard screams capture the early evening breeze.

Alpine Bob ignores her. Suddenly he's lightning quick as he grabs my belt buckle and jerks me to the ground. Instincts from my high school wrestling days instantly kick in. Capitalizing on Alpine's momentum, I am able to use an instinctive clutch hold on him. I hit the ground and continue to roll, easily pulling the mad comic over, then under me.

"Calm down," I yell directly into his face. "This won't get us anywhere."

Breaking an arm free, Bob tosses a fist into my chest.

"Screw you, bastard." I feel a thud but no pain, at least not yet. "You asked for it." I punch his midsection. This damn construction worker toughened gritty, leathery bastard, doesn't seem to feel a thing.

How it happens, I don't know. But suddenly I'm flat on my back with Bob straddling me. His fist lands on the side of my shoulder.

"I've been hell-raising a long time, you S.O.B," he screams. "You don't think you can beat me, do you?" He delivers a fist to my jaw.

Angrier now, I stop his next blow by catching his wrist, then jerk his arm with a snap turn. I manage to turn him on his back. Instinctively I want to punch him in the nuts, but I have second thoughts on that.

Whatever the comic was drinking has numbed his senses.

A ripping sound reaches me. I hope it isn't my clothes.

Alpine punches my gut, then rolls over on top of me again. All I can do is grab hold and try to continue to roll. Locked together, we toss and turn across the parking lot. Pavement and gravel flow off us. I find myself on the bottom again. Then suddenly, he pulled off of me.

Looming over the both of us, as if master of the scene, stands the Marine Corporal comic Bill Michaels. "Break it up, break it up, guys!"

He easily pins the struggling, drunken comic back to the restaurant wall by the shoulders. "You guys shouldn't be doing this." Alpine continues to struggle. "Quit it! Relax, Alpine. What's the matter with you?"

"Well, if it isn't the Marines coming to save his ass," Alpine jeers. "I'm going to get that sonofabitch. Let me go."

"Not until you calm down," Bill orders.

I stand up slowly, straightening out my clothes. My jaw and face throb. "Get out of here, Alpine. Get the hell out of here." I can't believe I'm wiping sweat, dirt and blood from my face. "I never want to see you—never want to hear or know anything about you—ever again!"

Maggie clutches at Alpine's arm. "Come on, darling," she soothes as he knocks her hand away. "Let's get out of here. You don't need this." Grabbing his hand, she tugs at him.

The Marine carefully releases the drunk comic to her. Saying nothing, Alpine glares at me as he walks away.

Bill stands between us until they disappear around the front of the restaurant. We follow.

Parked in front with its door still open is the taxi that brought my lady friend. I'm glad she's nowhere to be seen.

The cabbie, waiting by the open door, impatiently studies his watch. I know what he's waiting for.

Reaching for my wallet, relieved it's still there, I pull out a twenty. "Hey," I say to him. "I'm paying you. Come over here." I want to stay as far away from Alpine as possible. As I hand the cabbie a Jackson, another thought enters my mind. I pull out another twenty. "Take those two anywhere. Just get them the hell out of here."

"Okay Alpine, you heard Ronn," Bill commands. "Get in the cab and get out of here."

Alpine and Maggie slump into the cab.

"And ma'am, take care of him." Bill closes the cab door behind her while giving Alpine a dirty look.

My mind snaps back to the present. There's a show going on inside and, oh God, as its producer, I'm physically wrecked and emotionally embarrassed. My show's in progress, for God's sake. I have to get myself together!

I ponder life as I pace through the entrance of the Chinatown's grotto. I concentrate on the mesmerizing waterfall's soothing, flowing water as it gently trickles into the waiting pond. I again enjoy its relaxing power over me. I find a bench.

Bill Michaels sits next to me. "You did what you had to, man," he says.

"That doesn't make it right. I should have controlled myself better." I know my guilt is showing.

"I don't know why you think what you did was so bad. You did what a lot of people wanted to do to that guy for a long time. I'm surprised you put up with him as long as you did," Bill adds.

"Well, it's all over now. I meant it when I said I never wanted to see him again. He's been an embarrassment once too often. I don't care if he's a good comic or not."

"All I know," Bill says, ". . . is that when I got off stage, I was looking for you in the lobby. His woman came in crying all hysterical. She dragged me outside where you two guys were rolling around on the pavement. I bet you're glad I did. You looked like you needed help," he teased, smiling.

"All I know is we're both going to be hurting. He will come when the liquor wears off. Wait, I've got a show to oversee." I exercise my sore jaw and my aching shoulders. "And, if I'm not mistaken, there's a lady waiting for me."

I slap the marine's back. "Thank you, I appreciate your help. Let's catch a comedy show!" Standing, I know a bourbon and seven will go a long way. Wiping the remaining dirt from my clothes, I swing open the glass entrance doors.

Chapter Five

Only a waitress occupies the cash register. Glancing past the green tiled archway entrance to the showroom, I can see Lee Parks on stage pouring milk down the front of some audience volunteer's shirt. On second glance, I recognize the volunteer. It's Peterson, the KKOB FM reporter I gave an interview to a little while ago. I smile, because I knew better.

"I'm going inside to sit down with the buds," the Marine says.

"Hey, man! Thanks again. Keep up the good work." I add a relaxed laugh. It's a funny thing, I think with a smile on my face. Suddenly, a great weight lifts off my shoulders. The Alpine matter is settled.

The reporter's face on stage echoes his shock. I watch from the center of the lobby.

"Hello, Ronnie." A seductive female voice originates from behind me. It's a voice I never expected to hear again. I glance back. Sure enough, it's Linda. It's been many months since I've seen her. Instant memories flood back.

A broad smile highlights her extra-white teeth. Long blonde hair frames her face and flows to the top of her tanned shoulders. A low-cut pink blouse accentuates her petite frame.

"How are you, Linda?" I can't help my polite coldness.

"It's been a while since I've seen one of your shows," she says. "I needed some laughs. So, I knew just where to come. Didn't I?"

"We have a topnotched laugh fest tonight," I reply.

"I've been watching it. I like your magician," she coos.

Trying to think of something to say, I find myself stammering. "Are you still selling flowers?" Last I knew, she worked for a flower outfit that sends ladies from nightclub to nightclub selling roses. That's how we met. She had come into another hotel lounge where I had a show.

"Yes, and I'm still going to school." She pauses as she steps closer. "It's been a while. Why haven't you called? I haven't heard from you. I thought we had something."

As far as I'm concerned, I had reason to stop calling her. When we were dating, we actually weren't. We were just plain making monkey love regularly.

Months ago

One night I went over to her apartment unexpectedly. Both Linda and her roommate's cars were in the driveway, but no one answered the doorbell. I persisted for a couple more minutes without an answer.

Finally, the door opened a crack. Linda's roommate Susan smiled behind the open length of door chain. I was pleased to see her dripping wet with only a bath towel hugging her petite curves.

Her wet, frisky, red hair, (I've always had a thing for redheads), showed that I was interrupting her shower.

"Hi, Susy! How's the young lady?" I smiled.

"Linda is out of town," she said quickly. "Her note said only that she'd be back in a couple of days."

"Well . . . can I leave a message? Like my own personal note to pin to your bulletin board?"

"Sure, come on in." She walks away from the open door. "Excuse the mess. I'm moving out today. Got a flight attendant job with Southwest Airlines—I start out of Phoenix tomorrow night."

Her excitement was apparent. As I maneuvered around half-filled packing boxes, Susan's long haired, shirtless boyfriend, Hank, came out of the bedroom snapping up the front of his tight, worn blue jeans. His wild and wavy red hair was also wet. Two wet redheads, I remember thinking. Go figure!

With Susan in her bedroom dressing, Hank started talking. "We won't be double dating any more, now that we're moving to Phoenix. For that matter, we'll probably never see each other again." Hank sounded as if he was thinking out loud.

Stepping into the kitchenette area, I finally find a piece of paper and pencil. I jotted a note for Linda: "I want to take you to dinner at the top of the mountain. We'll take the tram. Afterward, we can cuddle with the view of the city, Ronnie." While pinning my note to the bulletin board, I couldn't help but notice an autographed head shot of the chiseled, good looks of my past week's headliner. That bastard was staring back at me!

Hank continued, "I'm going to miss Albuquerque. Susan and I are going to live together until I get a job in the new town. I wonder what it'll be like."

I didn't care what this guy was saying. All I saw was what was on the middle of the bulletin board. An 8 x 10 black and white glossy publicity photograph of Jack Pullim, the Hollywood comic I had brought in this past week. The autographed photo read, "Sweetheart, I cherished our special moments this week. LUV JACK."

I thought once I had paid this Jack-off his weekly talent fee I'd be rid of him. That was days ago, and I figured it was the last I'd ever have to see him. Bottom line, his act sucked. I never had so many complaints about any other act. Paying him was like dropping eight crisp one-hundred-dollar bills, one by one, down the toilet. I actually felt duped, embarrassed for hiring him and, because I'd promoted and hyped him up, felt he had misrepresented his credentials to me. All the negative critiques kept echoing in my head. Plus, his cocky attitude made me dislike him from day one. I knew that Linda was fascinated with guys who made a living on the stage. That's why she and I got along so well.

Also, it wasn't hard to notice that she didn't like the female comics. She didn't even want to meet Silver Vega.

Then the bomb hit. Hank noticed my attention on the photo. "Apparently Linda went off with him to his next gig," he said, nodding toward it. "I heard something about El Paso when he picked her up this morning and about having dinner tonight in Mexico." He buttoned his flannel shirt. "Said she didn't know how long she'd be gone and didn't care."

My stomach knotted at the realization that a girl I liked and cared for was a . . . a . . . a groupie! I seldom appreciate them, especially one that would go off with that S.O.B. The urge to see her again ceased at that moment. Even the thought of holding her svelte body in my arms was repulsive. I wanted to put my fist through that guy's mug on the bulletin board.

It was that moment I put Linda out of my mind. What she did with her life was her business. I couldn't help it if it affected my opinion of her.

Currently

Oh, yeah. I'm now on the spot, standing in the lobby of a Chinese restaurant. My show is underway, and my face is throbbing. I don't want to answer her despite the pressure I feel as I gaze into her sparkling eyes.

Then a hand grasps mine. I turn around to see Heather smile. Her fluffy red crimson hair flows about her bare shoulders. A snug-fitting blue and white tank top highlights pert ample breasts. A short, white skirt accentuates her toned, twenty-one-year-old body.

She says, "There you are, sweetie."

Happy to avoid Linda's inquiry, I pull Heather close. "Heather, this is an old friend of mine. Linda, this is Heather. Heather," I nod, "Linda."

Heather's grip becomes firmer. "Hello." She flashes a friendly but formal smile. Linda's manufactured perkiness drains away in front of my very eyes.

"Hi," she says in a monotone, stepping back from us.

A sudden rush of background laughter overflows from the showroom.

"Heather and I were going to have some egg rolls and laughs. Care to join us in the showroom?" I ask, hoping she'll decline. I feel Heather's grip tighten as she moves closer, placing her arm around my waist.

"No, no," Linda shies away. "Why don't you kids go on in, and I'll be there shortly. It's Heather, right?" She looks coldly into Heather's eyes.

This brief, silent moment in time feels a hell of a lot longer. Linda's eyes squint as Heather squeezes my hand tighter.

"Linda, take care of yourself," I say. "We'll have a drink after the show. Okay?" I know it won't actually happen. I lead Heather toward the showroom. "You don't know how happy I am to see you, sweetheart," I whisper. And, while I'm there, I nibble her ear lobe.

Chapter Six

Quietly entering at the rear of the showroom, I glance back. The lobby is empty as the glass entrance doors slowly swing closed. We sit at the producer's table in the back.

On stage, Silver Vega is enjoying herself. This is proving to be one of her better nights. Even the ladies are smiling, which amazes me. Women are usually the first demographic she antagonizes. Her tight black leather pants cling to her petite frame as if they're painted on and she glistens with sweat from the bright stage lights on the performing area. The tiger stripes of her low-cut blouse accentuate her well-endowed frame. She obviously dresses this way on purpose.

"That's right, Ladies and Gentlemen, I used to be a blonde. I used to be a brunette too, for that matter." She shakes out her shortly cropped reddish brown doo. "With the bad rap blondes have been getting lately, I felt it was time to change color. After all, face it, there has to be a basis of reality to all of those blonde jokes."

From the blondes of both sexes in the audience comes an unapproving hiss. None of them laugh, but everyone else does.

"Well, how can you always tell a blonde has used your computer?" Silver waits a beat. "White out is left on the screen." The room in general laughs at that classic old joke. Going with the energy, she smirks. "What do you call two blondes in a freezer? Frosted flakes. I got a million of 'em, millions of 'em," she teases.

The blondes in the audience boo while everyone else cheers and urges her on. Sitting in the far corner of the room behind the comics' table, Heather and I hold hands. I lift a couple of strands of her hair, teasing her about her blonde highlights within her crimson red. Both the egg roll steamboat and ice-filled high ball goblets on the table in front of us are empty.

Despite what happened earlier, I'm not feeling any pain. From where I sit, I have the optimum point of view laid out before me. Between the walls, from right to left, sits a full house. They are all laughing at a show I crafted.

To top it off, sitting next to me is a lovely lady I've grown very fond of over the past few months. Glancing at her laughing profile, I know I'm in love with her. I've never felt this way before.

"Why don't you give a blonde a coffee break? Because it's too hard to retrain them." Vega waits as the audience laughs. "What does a blonde say when you blow in her ear? Thanks for the refill." The audience is on her side tonight.

Through peripheral vision, I notice Heather studying my profile.

She leans closer to whisper in my ear. "I've never had a man who has shown me class before." I melt as she nibbles on my ear lobe. "I told my friend this afternoon that I'm in love with an older man." I turn my head to look into her eyes. "She called me crazy. But I need you in my life. Crazy or not, I love you."

As I kiss her, my eyes close.

Silver lives for this laughter. It is the drug that runs through all of our veins. Laughs pump up her addicted high.

Lee Parks slips into the booth next to me. "What's the scoop with Alpine?" he whispers.

I don't want to break my euphoric state of mind. "Let's talk about it after the show. By the way, you are doing a topnotch job emceeing. Thank you."

Glancing at Heather, the magician understands. He signals to William 'Weely' Cordova, The Lowrider Comic, that he's up next and to get on deck. Weely nods.

"What does a blonde say after sex? All of you guys from the same team?" Taking a few steps toward the radio news reporter sitting front row center, Silver runs her fingers through his thinned-out, wispy blonde comb over. His smile grows broader. "If a blonde and a brunette jump out of an airplane at the same time, who hits the ground first? The brunette! The blonde has to stop and ask for directions."

She glances over at Lee Parks standing at the side of the stage, so she fires off her best joke. "A blonde, brunette and redhead sit around a table to discuss cleaning their daughters' rooms. The brunette says she found a bottle of whiskey in her daughter's room. 'I didn't know my daughter drank,' she says. The redhead says that she found a pack of cigarettes in her daughter's room. 'I didn't know she smoked,' she says. 'That's nothing,' says the blonde. 'I found a pack of condoms in my daughter's room. I didn't know my daughter had a dick!' "

The audience shrieks with laughter. Through his cool and suave smile, Lee nervously waits for Silver to exit. She has the dirty habit of refusing to get off stage when she has a good audience response, like tonight. "Ladies and gents, my time is up, but . . ." she pauses, hoping she can get in a few more minutes. But Lee is poised to jump onto the stage to take the microphone—as he promised he would if this situation arose.

"I am Silver Vega. Thank you for laughing with me." Curtsying to her right then left, she exits the stage. I realize that's the easiest I've ever seen her surrender the stage.

Parks walks back into the spotlight. "Keep it going for Silver Vega, ladies and gentlemen. Silver Vega!" Parks claps to entice more of the same. Weely is prepped at stage right. A folded red bandana hangs from his torn rear jeans pocket.

"Ready for your headliner?" The audience cheers. "Well, like our producer Ronn Greco has said: This guy is being brought back to you by popular demand! If you haven't seen him yet, it's about time! Ladies and gentlemen, let me introduce to you William 'Weely' Cordova!" Leading the audience with his own applause, Lee exits stage left.

Dressed in clean but wrinkled jeans and a blue work shirt, Weely is lightly bearded with greasy, black hair. He approaches the microphone. He appears timid to the audience while he waits a beat.

"I have been working with Lee for more than a year now, and he still screws up my name. I'm not William Cordova. My name is Weely. Call me Weely. I'm Spanich," purposely over emphasizing his Hispano accent. A few people chuckle. The comic calmly pulls the neatly folded red bandana from his back pocket and slips it over his forehead. It partially blocks his eyes.

"I am a lowrider." Laughter builds. "I don't do any Walmart jokes." Weely Cordova wins over his audience. He adjusts the bandana half over his eyes again. "You know, people accuse me of stealing car batteries, jumping people. I can't see them. How can I steal their batteries?" Audience laughter shows that Weely has them in the palm of his hand.

Harry Jew has sent in more wait staff. They maneuver around the tables carrying trays filled with various beverages. I can imagine Harry's wide Cheshire cat grin as he stands behind his cash register. I want a piece of that action. Harry better watch out when contract negotiations come due. Just working for door receipts doesn't cut the mustard anymore. I need a portion of those liquor sales. It's only fair, I take most of the risks.

Weely shakes a prop can of spray paint, "I like to spray on these walls." He points to the KKOB news reporter, "Sir, do you know what it says?" The reporter shakes his head. "Neither do I because of this thing." He tugs his bandana. The audience laughs.

"It's pretty tough to come up here and be a Spanich lowrider comedian. It really is. I used to be white! Too much competition." More laughter fills the room. "It's tough!" He milks the audience's laughs. "That's a joke, vatos."

I peruse my showroom with pride as I sit in the corner. Every chair has a laughing, drinking, eating human body in it. This is a high, happy, energy-filled environment. But what really excites me is the lovely lady sitting to my right. She's relaxed, content and secure. Under the table I caress her inner thigh, then rest my hand there. She takes a quick nibble of my ear. "Later, I want to run my hands through the hair on your chest," she whispers.

"Your wish is my command."

The comic on stage remains unusually calm and collected for such a young stand-up. "The other day, me and my gang, Chico, got busted. We were cruising down the boulevard smoking a joint, drinking a beer. We decided to put tinted windows in my lowrider." Tugging his bandana, "But because of this thing, we put it in backwards. We couldn't see out, they all could see in . . . It's tough!" Now, even the usually placid wait staff laugh. Some even stop what they are doing to watch.

Heather shakes with laughter at Weely's jokes. I enjoy her smile and decide that sometime tonight, without an engagement ring, I'm going to ask her to marry me. I sip my white wine and know, while adjusting my sore jaw, that it would be the best thing I could do tonight.

Weely's wife, Irene, watches closely from the right side of the stage. She writes his material and has definite opinions when coaching his onstage image. With three kids at home, his nightly antics on stage have been his saving grace. He always wanted to be a comic, and now he belongs to the roster of comics I've nicknamed the Duke City Comedy Club All Stars. His day job as a printer at the morning newspaper pays the bills while the income from comedy has been his gravy.

A year or so ago I did a live radio broadcast on the University of New Mexico radio station, KUNM. Originally, there was to be a series of broadcasts. But despite instructions to the contrary, some of my uncontrollable talents experimented on the air with every blue, four letter word they knew. After that, the station didn't want anything more to do with the fledgling Duke City Comedy Club.

But at least one positive thing came out of that broadcast: it got the word out about the existence of the DCCC. One listener in particular was Weely Cordova. The next weekend, Weely, Irene, and a couple of their friends showed up and asked for an open mic audition. And the rest, as they say, is history.

That one audition shot Weely immediately to the top. His act was so superior, it towered over his established comedy colleagues. Soon many DCCC patrons were asking for Weely by name. Of course, his maturity had a great deal to do with it, being the only family man on the DCCC roster. The list of comics to date has consisted of bachelors, bachelorettes, college kids and one married man. Weely is the old man of the group while still in his early thirties. That makes me the grandpop of the gang.

Laughter continues to punctuate the room. "How many people here are married? Oh, everybody." Pointing to some empty, vague spot in the rear of the showroom, "Even those couple of guys . . ."

Again, Heather nibbles on my ear. Lee Parks excitedly slips into the booth next to me and whispers, "Is it true what I heard? Good job!"

Not wanting to get into it, and preferring to play it down, I whisper back. "We can talk about it later, okay?"

"All right. So how do you want to close the show?"

"Let's do a curtain call. Inform all our funny-boners."

Below the table Heather wraps her ankle around mine.

The Chinese restaurant audience fills the showroom with the loudest laugh of the evening. Every single person in the room is captured by Weely's meek persona as he simply stands on stage. "Well, it's time for me to go now," he says finally. The audience boos in unison. "Yeah, I gotta go. I was drinking some beers before I came on and now I really gotta go." Again, more laughter from the tired audience. Several women sitting at the front tables wipe tears from their eyes. "Thank you for coming tonight. Goodnight!" Weely waves as he walks off stage.

The audience stands with heavy applause for Weely as Lee Parks returns. "Weely Cordova! Weely Cordova! Ladies and gents!"

"Weely! Weely! Weely!" The Marines shout out from their table.

Lee Parks waves Weely Cordova back to the microphone for his very first standing ovation.

"You guys really piss me off," he jokes. "But thank you, thank you."

The audience applauds till their encore demand pulls Weely back up to the microphone. One can feel their laugh muscles relax temporarily.

So Weely adds, "Well folks, I have been holding it back, but I need to announce it now. Last Wednesday I signed a contract with HBO." The audience applauds congratulations.

"Yeah, thanks a lot, you know, fifteen dollars down, ten dollars a month, it's a pretty good deal. I'm surprised you guys haven't heard about it." The audience laughs and applauds. "Well, ladies and gentlemen, you have been a great audience. Good night." He walks off stage to strong applause.

Lee Parks walks back on. "Keep it going for Weely Cordova!" He applauds to egg the crowd on.

I kiss Heather on the cheek before sliding out of the booth.

"I'll be back in a moment," I whisper to her.

Heather's eyes follow me as I make my way to the side of the stage. As Weely's applause dies down, Lee follows up with the usual introduction. "And now ladies and gents, I want to bring back the man who makes our comedy shows happen. Please, a round of applause for the man the Albuquerque Journal in this morning's paper called the Godfather of New Mexico Comedy, the Duke City Comedy Club producer, Ronn Greco!"

I am greeted with warm applause, "Thank you, thank you. I just wanted to come up here to bring back all the comics that you've seen tonight. Please thank your MC, Lee Parks!" Lee stands next to me as hands clap.

"Keep it going for the man starting his comeback, Paul Lott!" Applause continues as the magician takes the stage next to Lee who shakes his hand in congratulations.

"Next, for probably the only Marine stand-up comic in America, Bill 'The Stopper' Micheals!" The table of Marines whoop it up as Micheals takes the stage next to the magician.

"And, of course, for that saucy señorita, Silver Vega!" A rash of male applause erupts as she curtsies next to the marine. "And, last but not least, your headliner for tonight, the most eminent lowrider, Weely Cordova, no, excuse me, Wee-ly Cor-do-va!"

The room vibrates with supreme applause. "Ladies and gents, we are the Duke City Comedy Club!" As previously instructed, everyone on stage bows in unison.

"Before we say goodnight, a reminder. As the week goes by, remember to tell your friends where you got your kicks. Right here, on Route Sixty-Six! Goodnight."

The room instantly goes dark. We all vacate the stage. Then the house lights go back on. Show ending music plays through the showroom speakers, the country swing band 'Asleep at the Wheel's' rendition. "Get your kicks on Route Sixty-Six. Amarillo, Albuquerque, New Mexico . . . Get your kicks on Route Sixty . . ."

Chapter Seven

Harry Jew walks away from the light and sound switches. His usual grin grows broader as a customer shakes his hand. "Enjoyed your show, Harry." He proudly accepts the credit.

Weely is surrounded by his newly created fans. His wife, Irene, tries to move closer to her husband, but is pushed aside by an audience member trying to talk to the star of the show. I notice her angry expression, but Weely doesn't. He is swamped by people who want to shake his hand or tell him their special joke.

Several crew cut Marines corner Silver Vega around the comics table. I watch her use her 'come hither' smile as these normally hardnosed guys eat it up. Standing next to her, Lee Parks is attempting to pack away his gear. A solo, long haired brunette wearing tight black leather pants, black high heels, and a low-cut white blouse approaches him. She holds a drink in her hand as she asks him about some of his magic tricks, and seductively places her drink's swizzle stick between her lips. He smiles and obliges her.

I feel a hand on my shoulder. Turning, I am confronted by a patron with bloodshot eyes. "Hey Ronn! Great show!"

Not recognizing the fellow, I greet him as if we had met before. "Hey, how is it going?"

"Great! It was a great show. Hey, I got a joke that you can use." Oh no, I think. Not another patron joke. "There was this fellow who walked into a bar . . . No, no I think it was a boy who walked into a bar, no, no it was a man who walked into this bar . . ." the patron started. I pretend to listen intently. "He tells the bartender hey, do you want to hear this Polish joke?" I try to glance around looking for Heather.

"The bartender says, Hey, I'm Polish. Do you still want to tell me a Polish joke? Do you see that cop over there? He's Polish." Heather has moved and now I can't find her without being rude to this patron. I'm resigned to the fact that I'm stuck. "Do you still want to tell your Polish joke, the bartender asks. See that professional football player at the end of the bar? He's Polish. Still want to tell your Polish joke, asks the bartender." I've heard this joke a number of times before.

A near full term mother waddles over to the soused joke-telling patron. She silently stands next him and takes his hand. Momentarily sidetracked from his joke, he turns to her.

"Ronn, this is my lovely wife Rhonda and our lovely baby." He gushes with pride as he places his palm over her swollen stomach. "Nice to meet you, Mr. Greco," she says.

"Congratulations, Rhonda!" I say.

"Darling, I was telling Ronn this joke that now I've, um, um forgotten. Where was I?" he stammers.

I decide to speed things up. "You were describing the guy who went into the bar who wanted to tell a Polish joke in a room filled with Polish strong men of various professions. The punchline you were looking for is: the bartender says do you see the fireman by the jukebox, he's Polish. Do you still want to tell your Polish joke? The guy says no! Not if I have to explain it ten times." I pretend to laugh along with my patrons.

Then, in what seems to be a regularly recurring event tonight, a soft hand slides into mine from behind. My smile grows. "A lady beckons folks, and I must follow. Thank you for coming. I hope to see you here again—and drive safely."

"Oh, by the way!" the patron interjects. "What do you think of the news?"

I have no idea what this drunk dude is talking about. "What? Reagan's bombing of Libya? The price of tea in China? The stock market explosion? What do you mean?"

"No, about that new comedy club coming here. The place on the other side of town is remodeling nicely. Have you seen it yet? They say they are going to bring in celebrities, too!"

"Can't say I have heard anything about it," I mutter as a knot grows in my gut.

"Well, I am very pleased to have met the man that puts it all together," the pregnant lady comments. "And I'll make sure we will drive home safely. I kept the car keys," she adds. The proud husband kisses her cheek.

"And again, congratulations," I tell Rhonda.

As they walk away, I turn to Heather, "Thank you for saving me, again, tonight." I prefer to forget for now the disturbing news that I just heard. Another comedy outfit in town is not good news at all. I take her hand. "I love you." Suddenly I realize that I hadn't planned on saying that. At least not in that way. It just slipped out. The only time I've ever said "I love you" to anyone is to mom and dad. But it feels so natural to say it to Heather. I gaze into her eyes then whisper. "Heather, I love you."

"Well, it's about time you said it, big boy." Not caring who sees us, we kiss.

"I need to talk to you," I whisper. I lead her out front door to the entrance garden. "Just as a thought, there is not a more suitable place for this question than here and now, in the front entrance of a COMEDY CLUB. Instinctively I go down onto one knee. She muffles her squeals as she covers her mouth with both hands. "As I've grown to know you over these past months, I've also grown to love you, darling. Will you consider becoming my wife? We can shop for your ring tomorrow and . . ."

She places her forefinger on my lips. "Of course, I want to be your wife. I love you, too! Yes, yes, yes!" She kisses me softly.

I take her in my arms and whisper into her ear, "We will have beautiful babies together." I can't help but nibble on her ear.

She giggles.

Chapter Eight

The parking lot has thinned out. Along with a few of the restaurant staff, Heather and I are among the last to leave. The radio reporter invites the gang to a piano bar for an after-the-show party. In reality, he's inviting Silver who then, in order to feel a little more comfortable, invites the rest of the gang.

Heather gazes up into the evening sky. "Sweetheart, look!"

She points to the full moon hanging over the tall, neon Duke City Comedy Club Marquee. In the middle of the parking lot, she pulls me toward her and kisses me while her hands slide slowly down my body. "Baby, I want you. I need you," she whispers.

"Your wish is my command, my lady," I respond. As the gang walks by, I raise my voice for the gang. "Sorry, folks. My new fiancé and I must bow out of the partying offer. Have fun, all." We wave goodbye.

Reaching my white Mercury Zephyr, I open the right door for my passenger. As she rolls down her window, I kiss her cheek. The full moon hangs over the neon marquee, full and beautiful. Walking around to the driver's side, I think I can see the craters in the face of the moon.

Heather smiles as she studies my profile. I wonder if she's seeing the black and blue, wear and tear that has recently left its marks on my face.

"I need you in my life darling," she says. I love you so much. We're going to be very happy together."

Slowly backing out of the parking spot, I shift the transmission stick and lightly press the gas pedal. She rests her hand on my knee, which she knows I like. Driving onto a side street from the parking lot, we roll toward the main boulevard intersection. Both of us glance up at the marquee just as it turns off, going dark for the night. At the stop sign I look both ways, then pull the Zephyr east onto Central Avenue—the old Route 66. We approach a red light, as it turns green.

Chapter Nine

Strangers approach my car. "Are you all right? Are you all right?" They shout at me.

"I'm not hurt," I say, since I'm not feeling any pain. Thank God, I must be all right. But . . .

"Darling, are you all right?" I ask as I touch Heather's arm. I turn toward her.

"It looks like a lot of people are coming to help." No response.

"Darling? Are you all right?" Still, no response.

I strain to turn to face her as glass crunches under my rear. She's facing straight ahead. "Heather?" No answer.

I hear fright in my voice as I shout. "Heather?"

Her window, knocked out, shows only ragged shards of broken glass around the frame. I can now see the car is wrapped around a metal light post. A street sign cuts through into the cabin over the back seat. The caved-in passenger door protrudes into Heather's side.

"Heather? Oh, my God. Heather? Oh, my God, OH, MY GOD!" My voice cracks, "Dear God. No, no. Heather, can you hear me? Baby? Heather?"

Strange faces keep sticking in through my broken window. "Are you all right, buddy?"

Not caring about them, I grasp Heather's lifeless body, try to pull her toward me and hopefully out of this fucking car. Carefully placing my hand behind her head, I whisper, "Let's go, baby, let's get out of here." I feel moisture, so I push myself closer to her and try to speak through my frightened tears. "Come on, baby, we'll get out of here. Heather?" I feel prickly pain around my arms, as glass shards cut at me. This same glass riddles Heather's side. The moisture I feel is Heather's blood. When I unbuckle her seat belt, her lifeless torso falls into my arms and I see a large piece of glass piercing deep into the side of her throat and skull. Her blood oozes out.

She's dead. I know it. I know it. I cradle her in my arms. "OH GOD! NO!" I'm screaming and I don't give a damn. "NO . . !"

***

Three years later

Once again, I head west out of Albuquerque over Route Sixty-Six, now Interstate Forty. Sun-filled, cloudless skies stretch over the panorama before me. Kissing the blue horizon, distant   flattop plateaus spread from left to right. This endless blacktop cuts a path out of New Mexico and into Arizona.

I'm on the road again for all of my weekend shows. Flagstaff, Arizona lies directly ahead and has been good to me. I have all the time in the world to think as I drive west on what is really the long and lonely highway. My mind often slips back to those events three years ago. Since then, life has been like my favorite ice cream: Rocky Road.

Mere months after Heather's funeral, my Mom collapsed from a heart attack. It was like falling dominoes around me. Questions rose from Heather's family. How could they lose a daughter and sister? Lawyers, judges, insurance companies, and the Lord were all involved. But at least after the trial, the vodka and beer chaser sonofabitch was sent up the Rio Grande to serve twelve to twenty-two for killing my baby and sweetheart.

However, in the same breath, the judge added a comment: "All evidence proves that the deceased, Heather Jerome, was simply in the wrong place at the wrong time that last night of her life."

Those words rang over and over in my mind ever since. Heather was in my company and the judge called it the wrong place at the wrong time. That brief moment wiped out all the precious memories I had before that terrible, black night.

Crystal blue skies perpetually capture the horizon, hovering over distant, jagged, orange/brown plateaus. Interstate 40/Route 66 cuts right down through the middle. A 65mph speed limit sign shoots by. I cruise at 69 miles per hour. All the windows are down. The dried out desert wind blows through the car.

My previous motivation to produce smiles, giggles and laughs ceased. Also, being a one man operation, I had no one to cover for me. The Duke City Comedy Club comics tried taking on the comedy shows. But no one knew the day-in, day-out of running the business. No one wanted to do the detail work. Within a month, the DCCC stopped shows at the New Chinatown. My other venues quickly followed.

Suddenly, after years of having comedy club shows throughout the Duke City, six to seven nights a week, I had none. It was comedy cold turkey, and I didn't care.

A few months after the trial, my mother had that heart attack. I knew it was my fault. She was sharing my never-ceasing personal and professional grief. I know the stress weakened her.

Then the drugs. Marijuana, alcohol and cocaine. But those three stooges didn't come anywhere close to deadening the pain, it was so damn deep. I couldn't kill myself physically, so I did it professionally.

Then, a new element came into play. The comedy void in town was filled. A new, neon colored, modern, full time, full week, professional comedy-all-the-time-type of comedy club opened in Albuquerque. It was an immediate success. Ninety-nine percent of the Duke City Comedy Club comic roster rolled to the other side. Each of them had to sign an agreement with the new club. If they wanted to perform there, they had to agree not to perform for the DCCC. It wasn't a hard decision for the comics. Only a few stayed neutral, mainly because they didn't like to be dictated to.

The bank of established and free comic talent I trained became a windfall for the new club and initially was their saving grace as they built up their patronage. Soon, the Duke City Comedy Club was funny only in memory and for many also on that new fandangled VHS tape of the DCCC cable TV shows. It didn't help my mindset that the new place was packing them in.

The only DCCC All Star who didn't care about the politics was the Eminent Lowrider Comic William (call 'im Weely) Cordova. Weely knew my promotional and managing efforts had strongly contributed to making him the most popular homegrown comic in the state and (for the time being) he stuck with me.

The morning sun finds its way through the driver's side window to warm my face. This seems to only ease my mind back to several years ago . . .

Chapter Ten

I-40 parallels the old decommissioned Route 66 highway as it cuts west through piles and levels of black-as-coal lava from the nearby 800 year-old dormant volcano, Mount Taylor, east of Grants.

Continuing west on I-40/Route 66, a desert brown and green roadside sign for the The Continental Divide, approaches. From my right side, the offramp rolls onto a dirt parking lot in front of a long red log cabin. A colorful sign over the entrance announces The Distant Drum Trading Post.

The Continental Divide runs north to south, from the Canadian Rockies to the Gulf of Mexico. Behind me, all the waters in North America end in the Gulf of Mexico, then the Atlantic. As I now cross onto the west side, I now know all waters flow to the Pacific.

As my tires hit that proverbial pavement, it became clear. Unless I was willing to work for someone else, there wasn't going to be anything for me in my hometown.

I had to get out.

One day, without a planned destination, I threw an overnight bag into the back seat of my '85 Chrysler Le Baron, turned on the ignition and aimed the car west on I-40/Route 66. I just wanted to drive, thinking only of the American saying that had motivated many over the last hundred years: "Go west young man, go west."

So, I went west, eye level into the sunset. I found myself visiting showroom owners in towns along the way. And, of course, the new form of entertainment, the stand-up comedy club, always became the main topic of conversation.

The old uranium mining town of Grants led into the heart of the Navajo Indian Reservation and the capitol of the American Indian

Nations, Gallup, New Mexico. On into the Arizona desert, I pass by and through the towns along ye ole Route 66, Holbrook and Winslow.

Instantly, the urge overcame me. The rock band, the Eagles, forced me to turn off into Winslow. I just had to find the corner to stand at to watch if that certain lady in a flatbed Ford would drive by. So, I found that corner and I took a photo of a street sign that reads WINSLOW before I took off again.

Then, there was the charming mountain college town of Flagstaff. Instinct said it was time to turn south. This led me down through the red rock cliffs surrounding the mystic resort town of Sedona. I continued south into the summer heat of Phoenix. My eyeballs start to boil in their sockets.

I continued on south into Tucson. Many stops along the way during this trip focused the possibility of talking stand-up comedy. The practice continued. I turn east onto I-10. Through the bleak southern deserts of Arizona, I know the Mexican border is to my right. Soon I am cutting south into Texas. The flat country greeted me with humid air thickened with the reek of manure. I pressed the gas pedal as I run the gauntlet of dairy farms that lined the interstate to El Paso. Off in the distance across the border, the grayish haze blew over from Juarez, Mexico.

As I put in the back of my mind that first trip years ago, I am now only thirty minutes until Gallup. My gut growls for lunch. My plan is to visit my client, the Old West-style hotel, El Rancho.

But my mind again now blurs back to Juarez, Mexico. A day, then a week in a drunken obliteration of time. The only flicker of a memory I have is that visit to a whorehouse. How I got out of there no worse for wear, I'll never know.

The next clear memory is when I cut back north, up I-25 into the New Mexican desert through the pass the pioneering conquistadors of four hundred years ago called *Jornado del Meurto*. Apropos, I thought.

The 'Journey of the Dead' runs through the land WWII Manhattan Project scientists used to test the first atomic bomb.

On that day, my timing was perfect. I just happened to be driving by on one of the two Saturdays each year that the U.S. government opens the remnants of the TRINITY site to the public.

I found myself standing in front of the black granite obelisk. This was actually ground zero. Right under my feet was where the first atomic bomb was tested. I stood there quietly for a long, long time, wondering about humanity's destiny since that moment in time when this was the hottest spot next to hell itself.

Where should I go now? If I chose to continue north, that meant Albuquerque and home. After some thought, Albuquerque sounded more than okay to me. Yet, I still found myself turning east, toward the Land of Billy the Kid. Albuquerque will still be there.

In Fort Sumner, you had to check out Billy's gravesite. I drive down the main road of Lincoln, New Mexico. And, sure enough, there is the very courthouse that Billy shot it out while making his great escape. I looked up at the 2nd floor balcony to see where every Billy movie shoots it out.

But then, the time finally arrived to go home. So, I drove north. To my left, the western sunset lingered a reddish orange over the horizon. As the black of night enveloped me, I pulled into town and smiled to see the night lights of Albuquerque, shimmering in the desert night.

Now that my memory is back to current, my eyes catch flashing orange and yellow lights in the rearview mirror. Damn! Sure enough, there's a black and white New Mexico State Police squad car on my tail, not twenty feet behind me. My heart jolts. Was I daydreaming or what? I didn't even notice the flashing lights approach. The digital speedometer still reads 69 mph. My heart races, then calms as the police unit speeds by.

Chapter Eleven

In the few days after I got back, I phone contacted some of the showrooms I visited along the way. I'd be their first comedy club show in their town.

Then the next challenge. Who was I going to hire to perform in these restaurants, resorts, nightclubs, hotels, colleges, theaters and military bases? All the comic talents I'd worked with before were contracted elsewhere.

The solution proved simple. Hire national touring comics. They would inaugurate my new name of the Route Sixty-Six Comedy Club Road Company. I placed ads in several national comedy industry trade publications and was soon flooded with head shots, resumes, and videos.

Talents from New York, Chicago and Los Angeles responded. Oddly enough, operating out of Albuquerque, New Mexico, proved to be a blessing in disguise. My office in the back of my Dad's house was centrally located off a main drag and I-40. This offered easy access to every road comic in the four-state southwest.

Since the days of Vaudeville, stage performers had to travel to different venues each week to earn weekly paychecks. Stand-up comics were no different. And, because of Albuquerque's central geographical location, it would become the hub of the American southwest comedy industry. Seventy-Five percent of all national automobile traveling talents eventually, as a matter of course, pass through the Duke City. And with weeks of work for them along the main artery of all this traffic, national notoriety increased for the Route Sixty-Six.

***

As I enter Gallup, I watch numerous, brilliantly colored billboards shoot by, one every 500 feet or so. Hot Dogs! Cokes and Gas! Stop Here! Say it real fast and they begin to advertise the truth. Indian Jewelry for Sale, Indian Moccasins for Sale, Navajo Rugs for Sale. Then, the largest and longest billboard (almost a football field in length) approaches in a rainbow of blazing color:

WELCOME TO GALLUP NEW MEXICO,
HEART OF THE INDIAN NATIONS

Behind the signage and off the freeway near the eastern entrance into town are numerous, individually multicolored American Indian teepees in a cluster designed RV Park. Three years later, I still love the sight.

Here I am, still hundreds of miles from my destination, Flagstaff, Arizona. Since, I have been making this trip weekly. It is only five hours to get to my Thursday, Friday, Saturday comedy club at their Monte Vista Hotel gig. Sunday meant another five hours back to Albuquerque.

In the years since that initial, solo, exploratory thousand-mile trip, I've crisscrossed the same paths countless times with the show. Since, a reversal of fortune has occurred. With seemingly many more now jumping onto my coattails, I now also suffer from competing producers following in my footsteps. My comics tell me I'm the only comedy producer who travels with his own show.

The reason is simple. I started out with performers years ago. To be on stage and to MC my own shows seemed like the natural thing to do. And now my clients, the operators of my showrooms, expect me to be present at all of these shows. Whether or not I MC, it's come to the point that when I'm pooped from all the miles on these bones and don't make an occasional trip, I'll book an alternate MC. While my clients always express concern that they are being slighted by my not being present, it's a rare occasion when I don't attend. When I choose not to be the master of ceremonies or MC, I'll be the Maître d'. Now I've become a recognizable figure in many Arizona and New Mexico towns.

This occasionally brings up embarrassing moments. People often come up to greet me by name and I have no idea who they are. After a while I have to admit not knowing their names. Occasionally, some are disappointed, but what can I do?

My stomach growls again as I turn off I-40. The first thing I see is a tall brown sign over the log cabin designated as El Rancho Hotel, my client. The extremely bright sun hangs directly overhead.

Parked, I scramble out. The front entrance isn't close enough as my eyes wince at the brightness of the sunlight. Without anyone noticing, a little steam emits from the radiator.

I walk in past thick, carved wooden doors into the lobby. The center of the stone floor is covered with Navajo rugs and lined with sofas and chairs with wooden arm rests. The complimenting side tables are illuminated with amber light fixtures at each side. Above, ethnically carved wood beams brace the entire ceiling. The far center lobby emphasizes a glass retail case displaying authentic Navajo turquoise and silver jewelry. A Kiva fireplace graces the far center wall, enameled bull skulls with horns hanging over it. To each side of the fireplace twin stone and wood carved stairwells invite all upstairs. A large elk head with antlers hangs over each of the curved stairs that lead up to second floor rooms. More Navajo rugs drape down over the wooden railing that encircles the lobby.

A second floor photo gallery surrounds and overlooks the lobby below. I have often thought that someday I'd like to add comic photos to the collection of autographed photos of Clark Gable, Kirk Douglas, William Bendix and Joan Crawford. Along with them are Fred MacMurray, Gene Autry, Roy Rogers and Dale Evans, Tyrone Power, the young

Ronald Reagan, Gene Tierney, Lucille Ball and Desi Arnaz, Errol Flynn, and many more. Apparently, they all stayed here while filming westerns from the Golden Age of movies through the 1960s. Maybe a separate wall could be added for my comics.

My game plan is simple. Call in for my messages before hitting the restaurant for my favorite Huevos Rancheros, red chile on the side, plenty of iced tea, and a slice of blueberry pie. Then I'll visit with the owners of this hotel. The Ortegas also own half of all the roadside turquoise jewelry, gas, coke and hotdog roadside stops between Albuquerque, New Mexico and Flagstaff, Arizona.

Soon enough, Willie Nelson's tune "On the Road Again" comes to mind as I aim the Le Baron back onto I-40/ Route 66, going west young man, going west.

Multi shades of color enhance the distant, prominent plateaus of orange, tan and brown. The highway weaves toward their center, ever closer to the Arizona state line. Orange clay, ten-foot gullies cut alongside the highway. Sparse green shrubbery spots the terrain. A few scattered puffs of clouds loft overhead stop short a few miles ahead, just over the Arizona state line. All traffic slows to forty-five miles an hour as orange barrels mark road upgrades. I can't remember when the road crews were not working.

Roadside billboards are still plentiful as the state line approaches. SEE THE AMERICAN BUFFALO, HAMBURGERS, FRENCH FRIES, COKES AT THE TEE PEE CAFE.

Suddenly the ominous, emergency female voice from behind the Chrysler's dashboard warns, "The Engine is Overheating. Immediate servicing is required." I look at the temperature gauge which has risen to the top. "The Engine is Overheating. Immediate servicing is required." All the other gauges read normal.

I slow the car and the temperature gauge cools but remains dangerously high. Damn!

After slipping the transmission into neutral, I coast to the shoulder of the highway, where I stop. Once out, I kick the innocent front tire and cuss under my breath. When I pull up the hood, a rush of evaporated steam greets me.

High speed vehicles shoot by, each creating suction that grabs and pulls at me. My eyes scan the vast distances of the far-off plateaus of this Navajo Reservation. The state line is not far.

I'll wait ten minutes to let the car cool down before pushing on to the Tee Pee Cafe at the state line. Billboards promote live buffalo at the New Mexico/Arizona state line. Arriving, I see corrals built at the base of a sheer, red rock, 100-foot cliff that runs parallel to Interstate 40, all containing the burly and woolly buffalo.

I remember this location. It was used as the backdrop to a Kirk Douglas movie I saw on TV the other night called ACE IN THE HOLE. It was excellent.

Neighboring the corral is the multi-level truck stop/cafe designed like a giant tee pee. My Le Baron limps into the watering bay next to a gas pump. Sweat drains from my body when I'm finally able to turn off the engine. I can hear and feel the steam pressure from under the hood. Nothing to be done but let it cool down and have the mechanic patch and replace what's needed. A thermometer on the garage wall reads 95 degrees. And still another 180 miles to go. Oh, what joy. I walk into the air-conditioned Tee Pee Cafe.

The state line officially marks the halfway point to Flagstaff. Even with mechanical problems, it's past the point of no return as far as I'm concerned. Besides, I'm expected at tonight's show, no ifs, ands, or buts on that subject.

As I sit down for an iced tea, I'm surprised by a memory from my Chinatown days. Somehow it makes sense. For every event in life there is a completely opposite but equal experience. We had one Christmas show road trip under freezing conditions and on the other side of the state when we crossed over from Texas into New Mexico during winter's frozen tundra conditions. Sure, I smile now at the memory. But back then it was no laughing matter.

Chapter Twelve

The clock on the wall pointed straight up toward midnight. Over two hundred people in the country club ballroom stood, smiling broadly to join in a round of standing ovation.

I'd been worried. This was my first show in a town of ranchers and farmers instead of the city slickers that I was used to.

My show tonight consisted of a stand-up comic, a ventriloquist, a magician and a comedy club show producer/MC.

I was basking in the glow of the ovation when crashing sounds of broken glass refocused attention from the stage to the back row of tables next to a tall Christmas tree. An obviously intoxicated grey-haired man in blue jeans and white shirt stood by himself behind his table. The edge of his tablecloth was caught in his fly. As he stood to walk away from the table, plates and glassware dragged along with him.

Seemingly unembarrassed, the gentleman detached himself from the tablecloth, calmly reached for his ten-gallon Stetson Hat and placed it on his head. He adjusted the turquoise and silver bolo tie around his neck. Only then did he unloosen the tablecloth.

"Merry Christmas!" he pronounced to the entire room. With a dramatic flair he pointed to the top of the brightly lit, chili-ornamented Christmas tree. "Beautiful Angel on high!" he said. Then he addressed the room full of people, "And to all a good night!" He bowed, turned and headed for the exit. The audience simply continued with their applause.

Chapter Thirteen

That applause was still ringing in our ears when we hit the road an hour later. A major blizzard was expected by dawn. Maybe we could beat it home. It was after midnight, Christmas Eve.

As ventriloquist Jake Pierson loaded his carrying case with his two stage dummies into the trunk of my Chevy Camaro, he smiled with the gut satisfaction of another performance well received. "We're hitting the road, Jack!"

"Let's stop and pick up a six pack," Alpine Bob demanded.

Jake and I smiled at each other, shaking our heads. Same ol' Alpine...

"Maybe I should call my mom before we leave," said the junior Houdini Bobby Blaine.

"So she won't worry."

In his gravel voice, Alpine spoke up. "Hey kid, you're a road pro now. You call your mommy on Mommy's day. You're going to help me drink b-e-e-r. Ronn, let's get a twelve pack!"

"We have to beat the storm that's coming," I said.

"You can make time for the brew," Alpine insisted, the last to load into my red Camaro. Flakes float down and around the parking lot, I watch the snow glow orange under the parking lot light. As I gunned the Chevy's engine, gravel spit out from the back tires.

The kid sat silently squashed in the back seat. I just figured he was shy. This was the first time he'd left home for a gig.

We cruised down Interstate 40 going west at almost 1:00 a.m., pitch black completely enveloping our rolling comic mobile.

Alpine popped the top on a can of beer. "Did you notice how much those rednecks enjoyed the show? Even in Tucumcari, on the edge of the fucking Plains, they need to laugh, too!"

"It's not hard to make them laugh when you have the assistance of two dummies to help you out," said the ventriloquist Jake. "My old man dummy is an act by himself. He drinks like you, Alpine."

"Guys, is it me, or does it appear that traffic seems to be pretty much one way?" I grimaced.

All silently nod in agreement. A muddy pickup truck sped by, kicking dirty slush onto my Camaro's windows. The snow was coming down harder.

I looked at the kid through the rear-view mirror, "Bobbie, I bet your mom was happy to get your call."

"Yeah, and I'm glad I called. She was waiting up for me. She said that there is a snow blizzard coming in. She warns you to drive carefully."

Jake patted my shoulder, soothing my ire. I'm used to dealing with pros, but this momma's boy was draining me. I slow the car to fifty-five miles per hour.

"Could you please turn up the heater," asked the kid. "It's freezing back here."

Alpine holds out a beer. "Here, this'll warm you up." Bobbie shook his head no. "What's the matter, Kid? Don't your mommy approve?" Alpine belched long and loud.

"Ah, jeez, Alpine!" Jake and I complained in unison.

"Blame the hops boys, blame the hops."

The driving snow increases so everyone in the car tries to ignore it. As long as forward progress was being made, there is nothing anyone can do, anyway. The vehicles ahead of my Camaro slow down and begin bunching up bumper to bumper. "Turn on the radio," Alpine demands.

"Man, I wish I brought my tapes." Jake snapped on the radio and turned the tuner knob through a whole range of stations, not a strong signal among them. Finally, he found one lone signal, a country and western station. Patsy Cline's "Crazy" came through the speakers. Everyone in the car shivered in unison. My teeth rattle.

. "Yeah, and it's an excellent tune. Did you know that Patsy's song is in every juke box in the nation? Crazy." I sing along.

An approaching mileage sign read Albuquerque 150 miles.

The snow falls harder and starts to stick to the car. Ahead, all the vehicles slow down further, so I slow another ten miles an hour.

"Shit!" Jake said. "All you can see ahead is a trail of bumper to bumper, hazy red taillights."

The blackness behind us is broken by a parade of headlights behind us too, I said to myself not wanting to add to the tension.

Suddenly, the rear of the Camaro fishtails to the right. Without thinking I correct the skid. The car settled back.

"Slow down!" The kid shouts through cold fright.

"Hey kid," I snapped. "We're speeding at a whopping twenty-five miles an hour." With a deep breath, I continued more calmly. "But boys, unless this snow lets up, we won't be getting home any time soon."

"My mom told me not to come on this trip," Bobbie murmured.

"Your mommy won't complain when you wave the hundred bucks in her face that you earned tonight," I said. This will be the last time I hire this kid. "Snow, snow and more snow!" I said to myself to get my mind off him.

The radio announcer flowed into his next song, "And now, ladies and gents, here is the new release from that cavalier country crooner from Taos, New Mexico, Michael Martin Murphy with his rendition of the classic 'Route 66.' "

"Here's an apropos tune," I said. "A country swing version, that's unique."

As everyone in the car nervously either sings along or hums the catchy tune, I look through the rear window. I only see heavier driving snow. Justified, silent, worried expressions cover my talents' faces. I can't see the road ahead through the iced windshield. Through my side windows I can still distinguish the rolling hills alongside. But the trail of red taillights grows.

"At this rate, we'll be lucky to get home by sunup," Jake said.

"Turn on more heat," insisted the small, shivering magician in the back seat.

I turn the heater knob up to the last notch. I was hot, covered with a big sweater and coat over my five-foot-ten inch, two-hundred and twenty-five pound, tense and stressing body. And this kid wanted more heat?

"Now I'm even more glad we stopped for the brews," Alpine states.

I ignore another swish of a beer can opening behind me. Why? At that same moment, the rear tires lose traction to lightly fishtail. My grip on the steering wheel tightens as I slow to fifteen miles an hour. Though we had gassed up when we left town, the gauge is down to three quarters of a tank.

"Maybe we should have stayed in town overnight," Jake thought out loud.

"After we paid for rooms, we wouldn't have made squat. I gotta piss," insists Alpine Bob.

"What the hell do you want me to do about it?" I snap.

I hadn't realized I'd have to babysit a kid magician and nursemaid a guy like Alpine Bob.

"Hey watch out!" Jake shouts. "That car ahead is stopping too quick!"

I jam on the brakes. The Camaro fishtails again. We skid down to five miles an hour. "This is getting ridiculous," I mutter. The driving snow was blinding me. Iced up windshield wipers swipe faster with little effect. All the vehicles in front of us link up, all the red taillights stop. "Well guys, welcome to life on the road."

"What are we going to do?" asks a nervous Bobbie Blaine.

"I know what I'm going to do." Alpine pops open another can.

I didn't even care that the can spills over its foam. I had other things on my mind. It's now 2:30 in the morning.

"For what it's worth, we're not alone out here." The procession of red taillights in front is as long as the line of headlights behind.

As we continue westerly, a couple of impatient pickup trucks behind us cross the median to the easterly aimed I-40 lane. Their intent is to bypass the parade of vehicles. After several hard bumps, the first truck makes it across the dirt rutted median and proceeds west. The second truck's back end hits a crevasse hard, stalling him in a deep breach.

"Some people have the good idea, some don't," comments Jake with his mean old man dummy laugh.

"Let me out now!" Alpine Bob demands. We could all smell his spilled beer in the closed cabin.

"Are you crazy?" Jake blurts out.

"While we're stopped, I might as well take advantage," Alpine says. He unlocks Jake's side door. "Open it!"

Reluctantly, Jake complies. Alpine kicks empty beer cans out as he forces his way into the biting cold. Jake slams the door shut behind him. "Too bad we can't just drive off and leave his drunken ass here," he snorts.

The cars ahead begin to creep forward. Jake quickly opens the door. Snow flies in at all of our faces. "Let's move!" he shouts. Alpine jumps back in, still zipping up his fly.

Building momentum, I steer the car forward.

Fifteen, thirty, forty-five, sixty minutes pass with the comic-mobile at five miles an hour. The engine and heater are running so hard that the gas gauge dips below the halfway mark. Snow continues to fall harder.

One by one, each vehicle in front of the Camaro work up a huge slick hill by spinning their tires to build traction. Most make it. Some don't and slide back down the grade. Finally, it was our turn.

"All right boys, let's go for the gusto." I pray silently as my foot gradually presses harder on the gas pedal. The rear tires spin over the packed snow. No luck. The car slides back down the hill. "Try second gear," Jake suggests.

I grunt acknowledgment as I try again. The car builds progress up the slick and now slushy I-40 slope. Our hopes rise as we climb up the hill farther than the time before. Then we hit an ice patch.

The Camaro loses all traction and slides back down the hill. I try to control the descent, but we end up farther down the hill than where we started. The rear end of the car, fishtails. We find ourselves off to the side into a snowbank. Again, in second gear, I rock the car back and forth. But we only slide even farther off to the side.

"Okay, everyone out, push us back onto the road," I order.

Without question Jake jumps out, Alpine follows by climbing over Bobbie Blaine, who remains inside the car.

"Bobbie, what are you waiting for?" I demand.

"I can't, it's too cold," he whimpers.

"Listen," I snap . . . "Are you part of this road team or not? That means helping out."

"Kid, get the hell out here and push," commands Alpine Bob as snow floats into his hair, eyes and mouth.

The kid, bowing to group pressure, reluctantly obliges.

Jake shouts back at me in an ominous tone. "Ronn! Put on the emergency brake. Get off the gas pedal. Don't move the car."

My foot complies. I push down the emergency brake. "What's wrong?"

The ventriloquist purposely speaks calmly. "You're six inches from sliding into a ten-foot drop. Take a look for yourself."

I turn off the engine and walk carefully to the rear of the Camaro. "Holy Jesus." In front of me is an easy ten-foot drop. The rear of the Camaro is hanging over the edge.

"Holy Saint Christopher," I whisper.

"I can understand why you've gained religion all of a sudden," Jake observes.

Bob takes a look. "Now I wish I bought bourbon."

Falling snow floats into all our faces as our teeth rattle. I wipe the snow from my face.

"Well guys, what do you think?" They stand frozen in front of me. "I can give this car a gradual second gear boost while all you guys push it away from this cliff, okay?" They just nod. I wipe more snow from my face. The traffic continues to pass us by.

"Let's do it, let's do it," a shivering Alpine Bob says as he moves to the back of the car.

Oh, so carefully, I sit back in the Camaro. Then gradually, I take a deep breath and slowly let it out. I press on the gas pedal while the guys guide and push us away from the cliff. Directing the car back onto the highway, I conveniently slip in front of a pickup truck. The comic, ventriloquist, and a shivering magician jump back into the slip and sliding car.

"We got the momentum. Let's go for it guys!" Again, I press the gas gradually. The rear rubber spins before taking hold. Everyone in the car mentally pushes the car forward. Anticipation grows as we climb closer to the top of the hill. The tires half spin all the way up, up and over the ridge. The interior of the car seems to expand with its occupants' simultaneous sighs of relief.

I take a deep breath. "All right boys, we're going west."

A never-ending procession of red taillights remains strung out ahead of us. From behind the steering wheel I wince at an unpleasant odor. "Alpine, you're not going to smoke a cigarette, are you?"

"Nerves, man, nerves. And it's not going to be that bad." He breathes heavy before coughing.

"Then crack a window, dammit!"

The other two bitch at him as well, before he begrudgingly rolls down the window and flicks out the lit cigarette.

"Thank you," we all chorused.

My gut cramps at the sight of taillights ahead and the gas gauge that dips closer to empty. "As we all know," I said. "Two wrongs don't make a right. So, what did two rights make?" A moment of silence takes over. "The first airplane! Ah!"

A belch rips through the auto cabin. "I wish I'd bought more," Alpine says. "All gone!" He throws an empty beer can out the window.

I could only shake my head at the littering deed already done.

"Look over there!" Jake points to the right into the snowy black distance where a complex of bright lights glow.

The crawling procession of taillights are all turning off the highway toward it.

"Looks like we won't be getting home any time soon, guys," I observe.

Fifteen minutes later, we reach the detour. Flares surrounded three National Guard trucks blocking I-40 in both directions. Troopers in snow gear, flashlights in hand, wave all approaching vehicles onto a side road. I drive the Camaro onto a gravel road.

"Well guys, looks like we're going into the army!" Jake says.

Chapter Fourteen

The National Guard Armory compound is surrounded by a chain link fence that disappears into the darkness. I drive into a snow-covered parking lot inside a fence to find evenly parked rows of armored personnel carriers, tanks, jeeps and troop trucks. I pull in, sighing with relief as I killed the engine.

The gas gauge borders empty. "Let's get inside and quick."

The front entrance guides grumpy travelers into the armory gymnasium. As wide and tall as an auditorium, its walls are shades of avocado green. Previous arrivals have already found their spaces. Male and female, National Guard personnel give guidance and direction to all.

Old style bleachers have been pulled back and folded up against the wall. The armory's emblems, energized Jackrabbits clutching thunderbolts in each paw, are painted above them. '419th National Guard Engineers' is emblazoned around the logo.

A woman dressed in BDU's, the Battle Dressed Uniform, sharply ironed for the event, directs the human inflow using a microphone. ". . . Until the snow packed freeway is opened in the morning, coffee and blankets are in front of this stage!"

"Did I hear her say stage?" I ask Jake.

Like a magnet, all four of us migrate toward her. Most of the human and non-human travelers already marked off their spots on the floor using their allocated blankets. An elderly couple clumsily lays out their blanket under a basketball rim.

"Didn't I tell you we should have gotten ourselves a room back in Tucumcari? But no. You wanted to make Albuquerque tonight!" The grey-haired lady's high-pitched voice squeaked at her silent and henpecked grey-haired husband as we pass by.

Next, we pass a young family with two blankets laid out. Two little blonde girls and a little blonde boy cling to their father as he pours a can of cola in their outstretched cups. Their agitated and disheveled mother reshuffles a diaper bag while keeping their little fluffy pooch in tow.

All four of us identify the aroma of coffee. "We're going to have to mark off our own territory. Are there any single ladies around here?" inquires Alpine. "Do you see any?"

We ignore him.

A middle aged, Navajo couple sit on the next blanket. Their complexions are riddled and sunworn. Silver and turquoise jewelry is laid out neatly in front of them. The woman watches over their domain while her husband carefully picks up a beautiful turquoise squash blossom necklace.

"Care to buy this for your lady friend?" he asks Jake. "I will sell cheap. We need gasoline money. Your lady will love you to bring this back to her for Christmas present." The ventriloquist stops and buys a more affordable pair of earrings.

I think to myself, buying the gas is no problem for me. Finding it is. Alpine and Bobbie Blaine stay close behind as our noses lead us to the coffee.

Flying out of nowhere, a beach ball hits me in the back of the head. As it bounced off, Alpine Bob catches it and throws it back to some children on the other side of the gym.

Finally, we reach the stage. Multi-gallon coffee brewers steam next to piles of Styrofoam cups. A note on the plastic box beside it asks for comfortable donations. I put in a five for my gang as I sip away. Looking around, I ponder the room and its inhabitants.

I look at the microphone on the stage above the coffee table. All these people equate to an audience. There was an idle microphone and an audience. Microphone. Audience. Microphone. "Why not?" I think.

71

I wave my comics over to the corner of the armory.

"Guys, what do you think about . . ."

I talk to the female sergeant before stepping up to the microphone. The sergeant stands nervously in the wings, stage right, while harboring second thoughts.

"Good morning and Merry Christmas, Ladies and Gentlemen," I start. The room still hums with conversation. "And for our Jewish friends, Happy Hanukkah. My name is Ronn Greco. And like yourselves, my buddies and I were traveling down I-40, ye old Route 66 . . ." My audience gave me half-hearted attention at best. "We're a traveling comedy club show," I continue. "So, like it or not, sit back and get comfortable, because we're coming at you, and we're coming strong!" A light smattering of applause reaches back to me as people start to divert their attention. "That's right folks!" I continue. "A comic, a magician, a ventriloquist and me! But before I introduce them, I have to ask you all if you have been keeping up with the time of the season?" I tried to sense my audience's pulse. "It's Christmas, and the spirit just keeps on going and going. Old St. Nick comes over on December 25th and Ebeneezer Scrooge on April 15th." A few laughs. "And good ol' Santa has to work hard. Especially to deliver all his toys and goodies in one night. But he still can't get any respect from runners. They always say, just once around. Big deal!" Stronger laughs came my way as more of the audience listens in.

The female sergeant's smile grows larger with the building laughter, reflecting her relief. I grin at her. Before I can speak again, the microphone and stand slip down, aiming at my crotch. I wait out a beat to emphasize the sudden embarrassing silence before pulling the mic back up. The auditorium waits for me with a touch of embarrassment.

Without thinking about it I say, "For a second there, I had a Dictaphone." More laughter.

"Well, Ladies and Gents, and all of us brought together on this Christmas Eve, the show has only just begun. It is now time to bring up your first act. He's a comic who is too far out there to describe. Give up a healthy round of applause for the bawdy one, Alpine Bob!" I exit stage right.

Applause dissipates into dead silence. The stage is idle for what felt like hours. Finally, a gravelly voice projects from the rear of the armory.

"Did y'all think I missed my introduction? I'm Alpine Bob. I never miss my intros."

Everyone in the room turns to see the performer make his way around the laid out blankets. "I am the only nationally touring comic from Mazoola, Montana," Bob says as he works his way to the stage. "And after you hear and see me, you'll be glad they closed and locked the gate behind me."

Even without a microphone, his gravelly tones project amply. He jumps onto the front of the stage, up to the microphone. "That's right, folks. I'm from Montana and this snowstorm is nothing compared to what we get back home. But no matter how you look at it, the only thing snow is good for is to write your name in it. And pity the fool who has any I's in there because they have to swing back and dot 'em."

A few moans reach Alpine up on stage. "Can any of you ladies write your name in the snow? If you want to learn. I'll be happy to teach you, after the show."

Typical Alpine, I think. My palms sweat again. It happens half the time I put him on stage. If there is such a thing as a comic loose cannon, it is Alpine Bob. I stand next to the National Guard sergeant in the wings. She's grimacing.

Bob pulls his pants outward. "What do you think of my baggy pants? You know what I wonder? Why do fat ladies wear white pants? When I get behind them, I feel like I'm at a drive-in movie!"

Those in the audience that like bawdy humor laugh out loud. The infants in the crowd cry equally as loud. I caught Bob's eye and point to my watch but Alpine is enjoying himself.

"I hate cats, but I like dogs," he said. "Have you ever noticed that everybody who has a dog calls him Rover or Boy? I call mine Sex. Now, Sex has been an embarrassment to me. When I went to city hall to renew his dog license, I told the clerk I wanted a license for Sex. He says that he would like one, too! Then I said, but this is a dog. He said he didn't care what she looked like."

The crowd in the auditorium laughs. "Then I said that you don't understand, I've had Sex since I was nine years old. He said I must have been quite a kid." The audience responds more strongly. But the level of humor is wrong for a mixed crowd. I signal him again to get off stage and again, he ignores me.

"When I got married and went on my honeymoon, I took the dog with me. I told the motel clerk that I wanted a room for my wife and me and a special room for Sex. He said that every room in the place is for sex. I said you don't understand, sex keeps me awake at night. The clerk said "me, too." Alpine Bob eats up the applause.

"One day I entered Sex in a contest. But before the competition began, the dog ran away. Another contestant asked me why I was just standing there looking around. I told him that I planned to have Sex in the contest. He told me that I should have sold my own tickets. But you don't understand, I told him. I had hoped to have Sex on TV. He called me a show off." Again came more laughs. Taking the microphone off the stand, Alpine works the entire width of the stage, striding left to right.

A very concerned Jake Pearson approaches me and whispers, "How long has he been up there? How can I follow that? Get him off!"

I whisper back. "Don't you think I've been trying? I've been giving him the signal! Unless you got any suggestions?"

"When my wife and I separated, we went to court to fight for custody of the dog. I said, your honor, I've had Sex since before I was married. The judge said, 'me, too.' Then I told him that after I got married, Sex left me. He said, 'me, too.' " He had the audience in the palm of his hand. "Then, last night Sex ran off again. I spent hours looking around town for him. A cop came over to me and asked what the hell I was doing in this alley at four o'clock in the morning. I said I was looking for Sex. My case comes up Friday." With that rush of laughter, I walk on stage.

Alpine takes one last shot.

"Ladies and gentlemen, thanks for letting me get up here and entertain for a while. I'm Alpine Bob." I was sure he read the anger in my eyes when he hands over the microphone. Keeping the energy going, I clap for Bob as he leaves the stage.

"Ladies and Gents, keep it going for Alpine Bob! Now, friends and lovers, comedy aficionado and fellow Route 66 travelers, I am proud to introduce your headliner, a ventriloquist extraordinaire! He has a buddy who came along on this trip, a polite fellow who is easy to travel with. You never hear a peep out of him until he shows up for work, unlike some other nameless individuals I travel with. Here he is now. Having performed in Canada, New York, Chicago and L.A., and now here, in the middle of Route 66, Ladies and Gents, give up a healthy, heaping round of applause for Jake Pearson!" I exit stage right clapping all the way.

Jake enters from stage left, carrying a suitcase. "Good morning, folks! It's different being here in the middle of the morning somewhere between Tucumcari and Santa Rosa, New Mexico. I just finished a major tour of all the big cities of . . . South Dakota." The audience laughs.

"Yes, I am a ventriloquist. Once, I was driving out in the middle of No-Where-ville, Kansas; I ran out of gas. So, I walked to the closest farm to call AAA. While I was waiting for them, the farmer showed me around. He especially wanted to show me all his animals. He'd say this is a cow, this is a chicken, and this is a pig. You know, like I was a little boy. So, I decided to throw my voice out of the sheep, 'What kind of farmer are you?' I made it say. The farmer's eyes got real big, and he started to run toward the house shouting, 'The sheep can talk, the sheep can talk! And the sheep is a damn liar!' " The biggest laugh of the night vibrates through the armory.

"Now, a little about me, folks. I come from a large Catholic family. I have nine brothers and sisters. I guess my mom wanted a large family and my dad just wanted my mom." Jake grins widely. "Now I want to introduce my buddy to you all. He and I go way back."

Opening his suitcase, the ventriloquist slips his arm inside and pulls out an old man dummy. The audience responds with oohs and aahs. Some of the children laugh.

The old man dummy struggles to clear his throat. "Well, it's about time you got me out of that box, Pearson. It was starting to smell like your old socks in there.

Jake sat the grey haired, overall-wearing dummy over one forearm while he worked the inner workings, with his other hand.

"How's it going Pop?" the ventriloquist asks.

"I've been pretty busy lately."

"What's kept you so busy that I didn't know about it?"

"I'm drinking and traveling again. Just got back from Canada."

"What were you doing up there?" Jake purposely looks surprised.

"Drinking. Canada dry," the dummy responds, silently laughing on Jake's arm.

"Hey, where are we, Pearson?"

"In a national guard armory somewhere on Route 66," Jake answers. He simultaneously turns the dummy's head to appear that he is hanging on Jake's every word.

The dummy then looks at the audience, all confused. Wooden eyelids open wider as he says, "Pearson here thinks he's a good ventriloquist, but did you see his lips move?" He silently laughs while bouncing up and down on Jake's arm.

"Hey Jake! Who's that out in the audience standing behind those pretty ladies?"

The ventriloquist pretends to strain to see his fellow traveling mate at his cue mark. Bobby Blaine stands near a blanket situated in the middle of the auditorium. On it, two long-haired teenage girls with letter jackets stretch out. "Well, don't you recognize him, Pop?" the ventriloquist asks his dummy.

The dummy shakes his head. "You never introduce me to any of your fellow Conestoga comics, you know."

"That's Bobby Blaine the magician," Jake says. "He'll be doing blanket to blanket magic as soon as you decide to go back into your suitcase."

"I bet he can't wait. Do you see those two lovely young babes he's standing behind?"

It really isn't his intent to flirt with the girls, so Bobby Blaine blushes. The girls giggle at their sudden attention.

The old man ogles the young ladies. "Well, Pearson, it looks like Bobby has plans for those two. Maybe . . . Do you think he can set me up with one of them?"

"Don't you think their youth could be dangerous to your health?" asks Jake.

"Well, if they can't take it, they can't take it," the dummy replies. "Oh yes, Ladies," he comments directly to the teenage girls. "A little advice. Watch that magician's hands closely. I've only got a ventrilo-quist here and look where he stuck his hand." The room breaks down into laughter. The female sergeant walks out onto the stage, as planned. She offers Pop a white piece of paper. "I'm sorry Sergeant. Remember I'm the dummy. Hand the note to Jake here." As the room laughs again, she hands the note to Jake.

"Do you want to read this note, Pop?" the ventriloquist asks.

"You gotta hold it out for me," the dummy says as Jake complies.

"There is a '65 Rambler in the parking lot out front. License number NM 23215. Your lights are not on and you are not parked wrong. You're just making the place look like crap. Move it, or some tank will," the dummy reads. Laughs fill the room.

Jake waits. "Well Pop, what do you have planned for this Christ-mas?"

"I'd like to answer that Pearson, but it's getting strangely bright in here, don't you think? Pearson? Pearson!"

The dummy starts shaking and rattling frantically on Jake's arm as the lights get brighter in the auditorium. From the dark of night, sunshine suddenly pours through the surrounding ceiling windows. It seems to blind everyone in the room . . .

Chapter Fifteen

Each comic road warrior experiences these adventures eventually. But each thinks that these are solo experiences. But in reality, these events are common among all show biz folk who have to travel to make that almighty paycheck.

But that old memory is forcibly dispersed as the coffee shop waitress places the bill in front of me. I pay for coffee, auto repairs and memories, put on mirrored aviator sunglasses, and now I'm ready to tackle the Arizona's Route 66 desert.

Welcoming me is extreme bright sunshine along with a wall of heat that slams my face as I step out of the air-conditioned Tee Pee Cafe. I get into the car after paying the mechanic's expensive bill.

Usually, I drive through this Arizona desert heat well air-conditioned, but it's been only fifty miles since the Le Baron overheated and as I-40/Route 66 leads past Fort Courage, and past the weigh station, the heat gauge slowly rises. Again!

With the approaching Painted Desert bleaching under the summer broiling sun, my palms are not the only part of me sweating. Do I dare turn on the air conditioner? Typically, I'd have a cassette tape playing. In this remote area, there's no radio reception, except an all Indian language radio signal. But any sound right now would only agitate my nerves.

I arrive in Holbrook, Arizona by pulling into the major truck stop that first greets all I-40/Route 66 drivers. I must let the car cool down again before I hit the road. I continue to wipe away pouring sweat.

Miles away and closer to Flagstaff, the beauty of God's landscape eludes me. My gut's wrenching as the temperature gauge rises even faster. At the same time, I feel my own temperature rise. Again, I pull the Le Baron to the shoulder, turn off the engine, and jump out of the car to raise the hood. Heat blows in my face, I wipe my eyes as I glance at the surrounding terrain filled with speeding cars, dry desert shrubbery and heat.

The clock reads 2:15, six hours till showtime. Normally I'd be there by now. Flag is only a couple of hours away. So, I decide to push it.

As the temperature gauge remains high, I stay ten miles below the speed limit. The desert around me seems bleak. The slower I drive, the more I notice the dried out, Planet Mars red dirt terrain of the Hopi Indian Reservation.

A passing road sign tells me I've got another forty miles to Two Guns, Arizona. Can I make it there despite breathing in hundred-plus degree desert air? The gauge rises so I again coast over to the highway shoulder and turn off the engine. Other vehicles continue to shoot by.

Looking at my watch again, I grind my teeth. It's 4:00 p.m. Showtime is in three hours and fifteen minutes. I have to get to a phone to inform the Monte Vista talents how to proceed without me. This week's comics must have already arrived from California.

"The Engine is overheating! Immediate Attention is Required! The Engine is overheating! Immediate Attention is Required!" The female voice from behind the dashboard makes me want to strangle someone.

Many times I have driven by Twin Arrows, Arizona, and seldom have I noticed it, but now, I'm grateful it's here as I slowly coast into the first auto stop on the edge of town.

Again, for the countless time today, I open my hood. The damn mechanic was supposed to have fixed the problem. Damn him! This time there isn't any steam. The engine compartment crackles; the radiator is also bone dry. My anger matches the 110 degrees on the cola bottle thermometer on the gas station wall. A clock hanging above a pull handle cigarette machine reads 5:30 p.m. I stare out into the great and vast no man's land, only fifty miles away from my show. After a long, slow breath, I study the two, fifty-foot statues of red and white arrows angling into the ground. Their red pointed tips are anchored, embedded deep into the Arizona desert soil here at Twin Arrows, Arizona.

After thirty minutes of cooling down, I refill the water and add another layer of tape to the engine hoses. Five, ten, fifteen miles roll by on the road before the heat gauge rises.

"The Engine is overheating! Immediate Attention is Required! The Engine is overheating! Immediate Attention is Required!"

I swear every four-letter word in the American dictionary. Thirty miles from my destination and I'm not stopping. I lower the speed to only forty-five miles an hour. Vehicles in the left lane continue to zoom past my Le Baron.

My eyes flicker back and forth between the heat gauge and the highway ahead. The incline of I-40/Route 66 rises into the clouds, from the desert desolation to the base of mountain country as evergreen trees become more prominent. My car chugs up hill, then down the other side. The next hill ahead seems only taller as I climb up the mountain.

I almost relax when I notice the highway sign: Wynona Next Right * Flagstaff 15 Miles. I'm almost there. The car makes it over then down another hill. Pine trees become thicker and thicker, cooling the air significantly.

Halfway up the next hill, the car screams at me: "Warning! Warning! Warning! Engine is Overheating! Overheating! Overheating! Immediate Servicing Required!"

If I stop now, I won't be able to start again. The next slope is higher than all the last.

Using the momentum, I aim the car up the next hill.

Suddenly the engine starts knocking a slow methodical beat. "Damn it! Damn it! Damn it!" I pound the steering wheel with the palms of my hands.

I lower my speed to twenty-five miles an hour. It seems to take forever, but the Le Baron makes it over the other side. "Immediate Attention Required. Engine Overheated."

The knock in the engine is now more rapid and louder as we roll downhill. I want to turn off the engine, but I'm afraid I'll never get it started again.

My opinion on the matter becomes moot. With a deafening clank, the engine stops and dies. I can't even swear, my mouth is so dry. All the gauges go dead. All I can do is muscle the car over to the highway shoulder. 7:15 p.m., an hour before showtime, and I'm ten miles from the Monte Vista Hotel.

I push the switch of the emergency flashers. Then without thinking about it, I pull the garment bag from the back seat. I lock up the car. With a deep breath I sling the bag over my shoulder and start walking up hill. Instinctively, I stick out my thumb and wave it at the vehicles shooting by.

I never realized that these hills were so steep. More vehicles approach, out goes the thumb. A freshly waxed and reflective yellow Buick pulls over to the shoulder ahead of me. Running up to its passenger side window, I smile at the fellow behind the wheel.

"Thank you, sir for pulling over. You're saving my life! I'm going into Flagstaff and the Monte Vista Hotel. Can you give me a lift?"

"Get in."

As I settle inside the air-conditioned car, I pick up a foul odor. The wonderful air conditioning blows full blast. This obviously clean fellow, wearing a white shirt and tie doesn't appear to be emitting the B.O. Ah,

Hell! It's my body odor! What else could I expect after sweating like a pig all day through the desert?

"Thank you, thank you again for picking me up. You don't know how much I appreciate it. My name is Ronn Greco. Please forgive me, but I've been stressing and sweating all afternoon trying to get my car this far before it finally gave out."

He grins at me. "No problem, I know who you are. You can't possibly recognize me, but I've been to your shows several times. Boz Wright is the name." He shakes my outstretched hand.

"You've been to my comedy club shows?"

"Yeah. Right at the Monte Vista."

"Well, thank you sir. Thank you, Boz, thank you!" I can't believe my luck. The sun shines directly through the windshield into my eyes as it sets over the western horizon.

We pull up San Francisco Street and stop right at the front doors of the Monte Vista Hotel. It's only forty-five minutes before showtime.

"Thanks very, very much Boz. Again, you saved my life. Remember, your tickets will be waiting for you at the box office under your name for Saturday's first show!"

"The wife and I will be there."

Climbing out of the car, I throw the suit bag over my shoulder. At that moment, the lights and neon marquees up and down the street go on simultaneously, before the summer sun sets. I smile.

As I walk inside, the front desk clerk tosses her long blonde hair to her side, "Finally! Everyone has been asking for you and wondering if you were coming." She slides a check-in card and pen over the counter.

"Hello to you, Melinda. How is my collegiate scholar doing tonight?" I put my bag down. "Have all the comics checked in? How are reservations?"

She hands me my room key.

"We've been getting a lot of calls, that's for sure. Your comics checked in this afternoon and have been asking for you ever since. They're in the showroom now. Also, you have several phone messages. Two or three are from one lady in particular." She hands me the message slips. Placing the pink pieces of paper in my pocket, I feel sticky with dirt and sweat. The front desk phone rings.

"Please send a message to the lounge to hold the show ten minutes," I say quickly. "I'll be down after I take a shower."

She nods that she understands while answering the phone. "Good Evening. Monte Vista Hotel," as I head to the elevator and to room 404, the penthouse suite.

Chapter Sixteen

The elevator doors sweep open, revealing the entire lobby before me. To my left, Melinda, the only front desk clerk on duty, is still at her station and on the phone. The old clock hanging over the front desk reads 8:12. To my right, two travelers carrying in their own suitcases enter the lobby and walk up to the front desk.

Melinda is swamped by phone call inquiries and the two new guests waiting for her services. Yet she still finds the moment to whistle at me. "Sharp. Sharp," she says complimentary as I walk by. I'm wearing a yellow/green neon fab shirt with silver tie under a beige linen sports jacket, sleeves rolled up to mid forearms. After showering, I hadn't had time to shave, so my face now sports the trimmed Miami Vice look. I nod, wave and smile.

Straight ahead all the way to the far end of the lobby and down some steps, lies the lounge/showroom. Its pre-show music bleeds into the lobby and echoes off the walls. "Get your kicks on Route Sixty-Six . . ." sings one of my favorite groups, The Manhattan Transfer.

Three minutes to showtime. This hotel, built in 1925, still radiates the spirit of the many people who have also stepped through this lobby.

The music gets louder as I step past the dining room to my left and approach the lounge entrance. Each step down leads into a hallway with walls that display framed, autographed photos of some of the comics past and present that have played this stage. Taking a deep breath, I whisper to myself, "It's Showtime," and turn on my internal energy switch as I enter the showroom with a large smile plastered across my face.

"There you are," Sondra, the lovely bartender, calls to me. "We didn't know if you were going to make it."

Out of the audience-filled room, one individual approaches me. My headlining comic, Dave Lefkowitz, outstretches his hand.

"Glad you could make it. We heard about your car breaking down."

"How have you been, my man? Yeah, that car is still outside the city, stranded on the side of the freeway with its flashers going. But I'm here."

"I was about to start the show without you. I've got the lineup all ready to go."

"Great. I'll MC." I instruct, "You'll close the show. I'll segue up the feature act then intro you. You have your usual Carte' Blanche." Lefkowitz acknowledges with a simple nod.

Then casually, Tanya, my favorite waitress, approaches the stage. Though she had stage fright months ago, I've shown her that the waitress who introduces the MC always gets better tips at the end of the show. She grasps the microphone in its stand like a pro. Sondra snaps on the switch from behind the bar and bright lights hit the stage.

"It's showtime, ladies and gentlemen. My name is Tanya. I'll be one of your servers this evening. We'll have many drink and food specials, just ask me about them. But now, on behalf of the Monte Vista Hotel, I would like to introduce your MC for tonight's show. He is also the producer of the Route Sixty-Six Comedy Club. Please put your hands together for Ronn Greco!" She directs the attention to the rear of the room.

The audience erupts with welcoming applause as Tanya exits stage left. I enter the showroom from the rear of the room. As I approach from stage right, I shake hands with patrons along the way. I finally jump on the stage. With a larger smile and my arms outstretched, I step up to the microphone. "Friends, Flagstaff-ites, Comedy aficionados, lend me your ears. We don't come here to cry in our beers, but to smile, giggle and laugh! It's showtime!" Reaching for the microphone, I glance at the back of my wrist to read my gold Route 66 watch. Showtime. 8:15 p.m. sharp. I scratch the back of my head. "You know folks, I know it sounds corny. But it's true. A funny thing really did happen to me on the way to the show tonight . . ."

Chapter Seventeen

The first of tonight's shows is going smoothly, no hitches. Opening the show is easy. I've lost count of the number of times I've gotten in front of a room filled with people who are expecting to laugh at each of my words. Mounting a show is one thing. Presenting that show is another. I pat myself on the back for a job well done, so far. One show is going down, one to go on this two-show Friday night.

Dave Lefkowitz's political and hard-hitting satire on contemporary society is his comedy mainstay. His high energy act matches his comedy rebel appearance: blonde, lengthy, straight hair draping down to his shoulders, with blue jeans and a t-shirt.

My opening comic is Bart Levy. From Brooklyn, Levy's working his way across the country this summer. I aid part of his way by booking him into my various comedy rooms along the way. This kid comic, barely twenty years old, has been doing pretty well joking about his Jewish family upbringing.

I looked forward to introducing Mr. Levy, "Well folks, are you ready for your coast-to-coast, New York to California laugh fest?" I looked around the audience to see how much interest they are showing. I convert to my New York accent to my southwestern audience, ". . . direct from New York City! Yes, New York City!"

During Levy's thirty-minute set, I go back up to my room to make a quick phone call to AAA. It seems like moments later that I'm back downstairs, on stage and introducing my raging headliner. Apparently Bart Levy's act is well received by this Arizona college town audience. Every chair in the room is filled with college kids, mid-aged professional folks with earthy qualities as well as blue collar types. They give Levy sincere applause as he leaves the stage and I return to segue Dave.

Dave's act is familiar, and it fills the room with audience laughter. As I sit down on the very last bar stool in the rear of the room to oversee my domain, I feel the hard traveling day start to drain my energy. But before I'm completely washed up, I wave Bart over and shake his hand.

"Congrats on a job well done. Good show! Let me buy you a drink."

"Thank you, Sir," he says in his Brooklyn accent. "I really appreciate it."

I like this New York kid. He's not the stereotypical pushy New Yorker. He's young, with only a couple of comedy years under his belt but has been sincerely receptive to my occasional constructive stage critique.

"I liked how you picked up on staying in your stage light. Don't you feel the difference from when you let the audience pull you out of your light?" He nods as he takes a swig from his foaming glass of beer.

Audience applause and laughter continues to punctuate the atmosphere from the headliner on stage. Then it happens. A young, perky, shortly cropped redhead, with an emphasizing tight polo shirt and blue jeans sits next to the kid comic to order a drink. The letters NAU, Northern Arizona University, spread across her chest. Knowing better, I quit the shop talk. Why talk biz when a young attractive lady is in such close proximity.

Immediately, I hold out my hand, "Hello. I'm Ronn Greco."

She responds with a subdued smile. "Hello."

"And this is comic extraordinaire, Bart Levy!" The two shake hands.

"Has anyone ever told you that your beautiful hair matches the color of your polo shirt," Levy tells her.

Her smile broadens as she subtly slides closer to him.

My job is accomplished once the two start their small-talk conversation. I excuse myself.

The smoke in the room begins to burn my eyes, so I step outside for some fresh air through the front door. It's great to feel fresh, cool Arizona mountain air in my face. Cool air!

Leaning on the outside wall under the club's front neon lit marquee sign, I relax and escape momentarily into the night as streetlights reflect images onto passing cars. I fumble through my pants pockets and feel folded paper in a side pocket. Pulling them out, I read the forgotten phone messages that were given to me earlier. Now is as good a time as any, I guess.

One of the messages was from comic Dave Lefkowitz and one was from Bart Levy. Another is from the editor of the local newspaper entertainment page requesting an updated press release on upcoming comics. Then one, two, three, four slips of paper from a Georgette. Georgette? Georgette? Who in the world is Georgette? The last message states she's coming to the second show and to expect her. So, my curiosity will have to wait till the second show.

The laughter from inside filters through to me. My wristwatch indicates that Dave's time on stage is about up. Stepping back inside, I find him ready to closeout another effort, filled with smiles, giggles and laughs.

I'm met with a wall of the strongest laughter yet this evening. I know Dave is closing strong once again as he bows to his audience. The applause overtakes the room, and he exits stage left. I pass through the middle of the room up to the stage.

"Keep it going for Dave Lefkowitz!" I say. "Keep it going for the California Kid, Dave Lefkowitz! And while you are a it, keep it going for your feature act, from the other side of the country, New York's Bart Levy! Ladies and Gentlemen, thank you for coming to the Route 66 Comedy Club tonight. And remember, as the week goes on, remember to tell your friends where you still can get your kicks off of Route 66. I wave my comics to join me on stage; they are ready and do so. I place my arms around my comics. "So folks, from New York to Hollywood, you can always get your kicks right here, at the Route 66 Comedy Club! Drive safely. Goodnight!"

The stage goes dark.

No sooner does the first show audience exit, the showroom starts filling up again. Two sold out shows in one night. This day is turning out better than it started as I welcome two more patrons to the Monte Vista comedy showroom.

I overhear a male patron tell his date, "He's a very important guy. He's the producer of the comedy club!"

With a warmer grin, I lead them to the next available two top table. "Enjoy my show," I smile.

Next in line stands an anxious couple, yuppie in appearance. The young man's face is red and seems to be sunburned. His polo shirt has an alligator over the shirt pocket. It appears to me that he spent his day on the golf course. His young lady clings to his arm like a vice and apparently he likes it that way.

"Give us the best table in the house my man," he says in a patronizing tone. "Heard a lot about this place and decided to check it out. My lady and I are out to have a good time." In full view of his giggling female companion, he slips folded money into my hand. "We're out for a good time my man. Show us the way. You'll take care of us, won't you?" They both walk on by.

I smell whiskey on him and notice his bloodshot eyes. "Yes, sir. Right this way." I lead them to the same table they would have gotten without a tip. "Welcome to the Route 66 Comedy Club, sir. Enjoy my show."

"Your show? Will it be good?" the patron snorts.

Instantly I want to tell them that the show is gonna stink. I want to tell them that as the producer, I always go out of my way to put on a lousy show. But I hold myself back. "Yes, sir. Your ribs will be aching afterward with laughter."

"That's a good man." He hugs his woman. She looks up to him with her sunburned face.

"I'll send your waitress right over, sir. Again, enjoy."

Walking away, I look at the five-dollar bill in my hand and don't know if I should feel insulted or slip the bill in my pocket. I'm the producer for God's sake! Tanya is at her waitress station, swamped with drink orders. She always works hard to support herself and the baby boy she raises solo. I slip the fiver in her tip glass.

"That table over there requests your special services, darling."

She manages a smile while filling her tray with drinks. I walk back to the Maître d' station, and there stand two lovely women, one of which I now recognize. At last I'm able to put a face and name to those phone messages. She is obviously waiting for me and with a smile.

Georgette has long, wavy red hair that flows around her shoulders. The strapless daisy-patterned summer dress she wears hangs below her knees. Her shoulders are freckled, normal for redheads, I think.

"I hope you got my phone messages?" she says, apparently feeling I should know who she is. And I do, sort of. She has been coming in every week and liked flirting with some of the headliners. I reach for, then gently caress her gloved hand as if to kiss it in a continental style, but instead I kiss the back of my own hand, going for the laugh. She and her lady friend standing next to her giggle.

I take notice of Georgette's companion. "Greetings! Welcome to my Route 66 Comedy Club, ladies."

"Ronn, this is my roommate, Tasha Marshall. This is her first time to your show. I wanted to get her laughing again."

"Hello." She timidly offers her hand.

I take it formally between both of mine. "Welcome. You came to the right place. Allow me to show you ladies to a table." The people in line behind them become impatient. "Follow me."

"Didn't I tell you we'd be at the right place?" Georgette tells her companion. At a table in the middle of the room, she takes my hand, "Can you join us?"

"I'm your humble MC tonight. But I'll send over a server. The first round is on me," I say.

"That's lovely of you. Let's talk after the show," Georgette suggests, as she releases my hand. With that bright perfect smile of hers, she must have a dentist for a daddy. Normally, Georgette would look very promising, but the last thing I need to think about right now are groupies. But first? Several more patrons anxiously wait to be seated before I can think about this pretty young thing. Plus I still need to find a few quiet moments for my own sake prior to going on stage. I have to get the adrenaline pumping.

Feeling very comfortable with his audience, Bart Levy's energy is high. "Have you ever been walking around somebody else's house and without thinking, you just spit?" The audience breaks up. "I saw this lady the other day wearing a t-shirt that said that men are liars. I told her that she was very beautiful." Laughter continues. "She didn't believe me."

I always feel great when my showroom fills with laughs. Tonight is no exception. Purposely sitting on the last stool at the bar in the rear of the room, as far from the stage as one can sit, I'm glad no one can see me yawn. Despite the energy all around me, the length of day is catching up with me fast.

Bart Levy wipes the sweat from his brow with his sleeve.

"Ladies and Gentlemen, it has been a pleasure performing for you here in Flagstaff, Arizona. Back in Brooklyn, we never heard of you. When the Route 66 producer Ronn Greco said he wanted me in Flagstaff, I told him to talk to my agent. Ladies and gentlemen, my agent was out of town, and I am very glad he was. I love it here. And I look forward to returning. Thank you for having me. God bless. Good night!" He takes a bow and enjoys the moment of applause.

In no time, I'm back up on stage. "Bang your hands together for New York's Bart Levy! Bart Levy, ladies and gentlemen!" The audience obliges with enthusiasm. "Well, folks, we can feel the electricity in this room. So, to keep the energy surging without missing a beat, the time has come to introduce to you, your headliner. We just enjoyed the New York and East coast flavor of smiles, giggles and laughs. Now we cross our country to taste the flavor of the West coast. Direct from Hollywood, welcome him to Flagstaff's Route 66 Comedy Club. Put them together for Dave Lefkowitz!" The audience applauds as I exit stage right.

In blue jeans and t-shirt, with long straight hair down to his shoulders, Dave takes the stage. Energy immediately captures the room.

"I'm here folks, I'm here! Say hallelujah, Flagstaff! I love it here. Any dads in the audience tonight? With tomorrow being Father's Day, try being reflective. Buy him a present he can afford." Laughter builds. Through his loopy persona, "I love my dad. But last year I remembered Father's Day being in mid-July." He shrugs his shoulders, "Not this year. This year I have already sent him his present, a bottle of cologne and three ties." He waits a beat, "Hey, I may be a comic. But I didn't say I wasn't average." The audience relaxes with him.

The right exit of the stage leads me into a passage that guides me into the kitchen, then the dining room. This has become the standard path for all talents to exit the stage. I slide by Bonnie, the waitress who carries out food orders. Her tray holds a couple of plates of quesadillas.

The savory visual appeal of cheddar cheese wrapped with folded up and sliced flour tortillas, garnished with guacamole has an aroma that suddenly reminds me that I am famished. I haven't had dinner yet.

Avoiding the hustle and bustle of the kitchen, I divert through the adjacent, idle and thereby darkened dining room. The first round of echoing audience laughter reverberates through the entire area. I stand by myself and smile in the center of the room while simply experiencing the moment of folks enjoying my show.

To return to the showroom, I have to circle back through an idle hotel lobby. Energy quickly drains from me. I've had a long, long day! The semiquiet of the lobby drains me further. I sink into a high backed cushioned lobby sofa chair. Laughter resonates off these old lobby walls. Dave is killing them. As the clock ticks each slow second over the front desk, I am unable, even not willing, to keep heavy eyelids open. So it's simple. I'll just rest here for a few minutes before I walk back into the showroom.

Out of nowhere, I'm jolted back to the real world. Almost an hour later, reality snaps me into standing attention.

The sound of hordes of people exiting the showroom with boisterous laughter and talk wash over me. I've missed my cue to close the show and now, it's over. People are leaving.

I rush down the steps to the showroom—which is already half empty. Still, the fact that so many patrons remain, tells me that at least they enjoyed the show. Otherwise there would have been a quick exodus.

Plopping myself at my favorite stool at the end of the bar, I am overcome with embarrassment and shame. Sondra, swamped with drink glasses to wash behind the bar, hustles over. "What can I get you Ronn? Hey, how long was your headliner supposed to perform? He was up there for at least an hour and a half!"

"An hour and a half is Dave's normal time," I state in a matter of fact manner. But inside I'm astonished. Was I asleep for an hour and a half? The thought alone drains any recouped energy and even more.

"Well, he did his job. Our tips are the best in weeks," she says. "What are you drinking?" She doesn't appear to register that I actually missed the closing.

"Ah, no. Nothing for me, thanks."

That yuppie couple approach me. Well, here it comes, I think.

"Good show my man. Agnes, my wife here and I, enjoyed it tremendously. Your comic Dave is a find. We'll be back."

"Thank you, sir." They didn't seem to miss me either and still enjoyed the show? No one missed me? Have I gotten away with it? My God! No one missed me? I don't know if I should feel hurt or relieved. Sitting here, watching the wait staff work hard in their cleanup efforts, makes my exhaustion worse.

"There he is!" comes the voice of Bart Levy. He stands at the lounge entrance with a group of college kids. He approaches me, "What happened to you?" Before I can answer he continues. "It was a great show, wasn't it? Dave is a fantastic comic! An hour and a half man! And he had them in the palm of his hand!"

"He killed it," I agree. I've seen Dave kill many times before. "And you did pretty well yourself. Feel good about it," I add.

"Well, thanks. Hey, a group of us are going dancing. Do you want to come?"

"Hey man, normally I'd say yes. You know I'm a dancing animal. I appreciate the invite, but I've had a long, long, day already. I'll see ya tomorrow. Have fun."

He grips my outstretched hand. "Take it easy, Ronn. See you tomorrow. Late in the afternoon."

Watching the kid leave to join his new friends for the night, I remember when I was younger. I would have said yes in a flash. Coupled with being dead tired, they make me feel old.

I turn to see my image in the mirror behind the bar. My eyes lock onto Tanya who is returning to serve her tables, tray in hand carrying three drinks. She takes them to Dave, my headliner, who sits next to Georgette and Tasha.

"Sondra," I call. She turns to me. "I've changed my mind. I'll take a shot of schnapps." It didn't take long for the groupies and comic to find each other, I think. Sitting at the table between the two ladies, Dave is smiling wide, obviously enjoying the company of Georgette and her roommate. They attentively hang on his every word. Tasha laughs at almost everything he says.

Sondra places the shot of the clear liquid in front of me. "You look really tired, Ronn. You're making me tired. And tired I don't want to be. I'm meeting my dreamboat later."

I throw the shot of schnapps down my throat. The groupies laugh as though from far away as the warmth flows through me. There is no more doubt about it. It's time to hit the sack. "Take care baby," I mumble to Sondra. "I'll see ya tomorrow night. Enjoy your rendezvous."

Groggy, I pace myself through the lobby to push the up button on the elevator. A new graveyard front desk clerk is on duty. I don't know his name.

"Mr. Greco. You have a phone message here about your car being delivered to a garage," the desk clerk yells.

The elevator doors open. "Thanks. I'll pick it up in the morning," I mumble back.

Finally, the doors open and I stumble down the hallway to the door with the JOHN WAYNE name plate on it. A cool mountain breeze greets me inside from the window I left open. The only light in the room comes from the blinking red neon sign hanging right outside the window. It alternates and flashes. The curtains lightly sway in the cool breeze.

All I can see through the flashing reddish room is my plush bed. Bolting the door closed behind me, I fall face down on the bedspread, fully clothed. As far as I'm concerned, this long day has officially ended.

Chapter Eighteen

It starts up from my feet, then up my legs and over my rear end. I feel the warmth rise up my spine and up the back of my skull. As I turn over, the warmth settles on my eye lids. I open my eyes to see the rising sun shining through the window, yet I remain in place, not wanting to move a muscle.

From only two streets away I hear the whistle, followed by the rumble of the 7:30 a.m. Amtrak that has never been late as long I've been coming to Flagstaff, Arizona.

I know I have a lot to do today, but my body doesn't care, nor does it want to move. Sleep is so, so easy, despite the crumpled clothes I still wear.

Startling me, the phone rings. I choose to ignore it. Yet the damn ringing continues, preventing me from reverting to sweet slumber.

"Who in the fuck is calling me this early in the damn morning?" I ask myself. It's a major effort to get out of bed to stumble across the room. Like a phone from the 1920's, I grab the receiver from its side cradle and place it over my ear. "Hello!" I bellow into the funnel tube in front of the phone. My face is practically resting on the phone's push-button dialing pad in front of my nose. This phone has to figure out what decade it's in, I think.

"Hello. Mr. Greco? This is Jeff over at Flagstaff Garage. Is this your Chrysler Le Baron that AAA towed in last night?" The distant voice sounded official.

"Oh, yeah," I sigh as I'm brought back to the real world. My attitude quickly changes. "Yes sir, that's me. What's the news?"

"Sad to report to you sir, but you have a completely blown and burnt out engine." The distant voice is matter of fact.

"Okay. Okay." I knew it was going to be bad. "Okay, how much to fix it?"

"Sir, you don't seem to understand. The engine is completely blown out. The pistons are fused, there isn't any water in the engine, and it's completely burnt out."

I need the car to get home. All I really want to know is will it be fixed today. "Okay. Okay. How long will it take to fix? I need it by tomorrow."

"Well, sir. You know that you need a whole new engine, don't you?"

"A new engine?!" This bolt of lightning wakes me up. "New engine?! It's that bad? Damn it." The realization hits. "Blown engine?"

"Yes sir. And with this turbo charger on it, you'll have a hard time replacing it in this town."

I fight off an early morning yawn, "Sir, is it, uh. Jeff? Jeff, I'll give you a call right back after I have my morning shower and coffee," I say, hanging up. I take a step toward the shower. But the sight of the pillow on the bed seduces me back with ease. I'll simply worry about things later. As my head snuggles into the pillow, there is no problem dozing off again.

It seems like no time at all when the damn phone rings again, over and over. My baby browns open to view the travel alarm clock on the bedside table. I drag my body across the hotel room floor, again. I know that this room is the best in the hotel. But this phone is a pain in the. . . The phone begins to ring again. I juggle the receiver to my ear. "Hello."

"Hello? Ronnie?" A soft young lady's voice inquires.

My sleep-groped mind doesn't register the voice. I yawn widely, "Yeah, uh huh. This is Ronn Greco."

"This is Georgette! Georgette Collins! Did I wake you?"

"I had to get up. Thank you for being my alarm clock." My mind's eye tries to tune into the nuances of her voice while placing it with a face.

"I wondered why you didn't come over to the table after the show. Then finally Dave told me what you went through yesterday."

Through a foggy vagueness I recall the face of the redhead groupie. "I was so tired I slept like a log, that's for sure." I want to keep the positive edge about it.

A sudden gust of wind blows hard through the open window. The table lamp from beside the bed falls to the floor.

"Who was that?" she asks. "Is someone with you? Did I disturb you?" Strange curiosity overtones lace her voice.

"Naw, naw. That was just the wind through the window knocking down a table lamp." She sounds relieved. "I wished you had come over to the table last night. Came to see you as much as your show, you know."

Now it registers together. I now place the voice with the face with red hair, along with the name, "Well, dear . . . I was so beat last night, I had to hit the sack hard." I purposely want to state her name, "Georgette, I am surprised and very much complimented that you're calling me. You're the best way to wake up this morning, I'll tell you," is all I can think to say.

"Wasn't Dave and your other comic great last night?"

"I've seen Dave's show several times. He never fails."

"I wished you would have come over to talk afterward," she says again. "I came home after the show still wanting to party. Dave and Tasha must have hit it off. She just called me from your hotel minutes ago. Probably from Dave's room. They want to go down to Sedona today and they want to know if we'd like to come along?"

I do not answer and after a moment, she continues.

"Would you like to go with me to Sedona, you comedy showman?"

I have this phobia about groupies, "Oh, I'm sorry. Normally, I'd say yes but . . ."

"We could leave in a couple of hours," she interrupts. "It's only thirty minutes south. We could have lunch there and spend the afternoon getting to know each other."

"You don't understand. Normally I would say yes in a second, but my wheels are in the garage." I am depressed by the thought.

"No problem," she says. "I'll drive. I'm supposed to pick up those guys at 10:30 anyway. If you don't come, I'll end up flittering away the first free day from school I've had in some time . . . Besides, you don't want me to be third wheel with the other two, do you?"

She's trapped me. Why not, I think. Otherwise I'll be brooding over my car all day long. "Well darling, I'd be a fool to turn down a lovely lady's invitation like that. Let's go for it. See you in the lobby."

I hang up, surprised. A lady is pursuing me for a change. Suddenly I feel great.

***

The plain office clock over the lobby's front desk shows 10:25 as I step out of the elevator. AAA is great insurance! With one phone call, I arranged a tow. My comic mobile Le Baron will be sent back to Albuquerque where I'll worry about it there. I'll take my first Amtrak ride Sunday at 7:00 a.m. I will be back home Sunday afternoon.

As I wait for my lady chauffeur, the arrow above the elevator doors moves slowly down to this first floor. As the doors pull open, my headliner and his groupie step out into the lobby. She breaks away to the lobby phone, so Dave approaches me.

"She's an archaeology student at Northern Arizona University," Dave tells me. "And she just broke up with her boyfriend too."

So I say, "And I bet she made up for it by digging up your bone." Dave laughs. "And if I know you, Mr. Lefkowitz, you got real Cro-Magnon with her too." With no denial, he just grins.

***

The two-lane state highway winds downward, south from Flagstaff through a national forest with high pines. Georgette's chartreuse BMW convertible hugs the sharp turns confidently under lush, towering forests. Flashes of sunshine cut through the tops of nature's creations. Its rays warm all four of our faces as we all wear Route 66 Comedy maroon colored polo shirts. The Club's Route 66 logo, in white, shines off our chests. Dave and Tasha nestle in the back seat while Georgette commands the driver's seat. One hand is on the steering wheel of the vehicle daddy gave her for graduation. She smiles at me as I sit in the passenger seat next to her.

"I love coming down here. It always refreshes me," she says. The sun finds another patch of blue sky to shoot light through, and for a moment, I'm very sure that my eyes catch a sparkle off her bright white teeth.

Modern log cabins border the road with rustic timber fences separating the neighbors. Thick forests of pristine green seem to freshen and cool the air.

"Erosion has sculpted this canyon for over 250 million years," volunteers Tasha. "Ancient Indians believe that Sedona is hallowed land. That's why many ancient ruins still exist." She wears sunglasses and a plain ball cap pulled down over her head. Her long black ponytail is pulled through the rear loop. Her khaki hiking shorts show toned, tanned and smooth legs. Painted red toenails peak through hemp rope sandals.

"Hey Ronn. Did you know that Tasha is an archaeology graduate? She knows of what she speaks." The comic thrusts his chest over hers to nibble on her opposite ear lobe. She laughs and hugs him back.

Glancing at them in the rearview mirror, Georgette shifts the Beamer into fourth gear then takes my hand into hers. "You know, I have been imagining this moment since I caught your first show."

I'm finding enjoyment at being pursued by this college coed.

"With all the comics I've brought to Flagstaff, you've introduced yourself to a fair share of them over these past months. I didn't think you'd noticed the show's producer," I tease.

"Who do you think I was trying to reach? I was trying to get to you through them. So I just decided to go straight to the source." She squeezes my hand over the stick shift knob.

Sheer dirt red cliffs appear off in the distance through the thinning Ponderosas. Resorts and motels become more common on the winding stretch of highway 89A. Warmer desert air wafts over our faces. The brighter sunshine ignites my passions. We pass through the gentle grasp of Mother Nature's pines and sequoias and into the shadows of all-encompassing red rock cliffs. "My God, it's so beautiful," I cannot help but say.

A jagged sandstone pyramid of layered orange, brown and red peaks rise on the right of the BMW. It is the first of many jagged stratum and plateaus that cut and shape with the winds of time.

"That's Steamboat Rock," Georgette says.

To our left, a helicopter pad receives a landing whirlybird while another swirls and waits to take off.

"They're lifting off to do fly overs of the Grand Canyon," adds Tasha. On the left, a row of pink tourist jeeps with pink and white striped canopies wait for customers. In the distance behind this business operation sit layers of colored plateaus capped off with endless blue skies. "That's a tour company I worked for last summer," Tasha explains while pointing at the peaks behind it.

"That's Elephant Rock. And those four coned-shaped peaks are called 'The Nuns.' " She smiles at her comic conquest. "I can show you some adorable, silent and so private red rock back country out there where a person can stretch out under the sun and nature wild. If a person wanted to," she adds.

"So, you're a tour guide too?" Dave leans over her. She kisses him.

Sedona spreads out before us. Tourist-oriented shopping strips, motels and restaurants with stereotypically dressed tourists scurrying around is all I can see. But behind it all is the panoramic beauty of the countless jagged towers of the surrounding plateaus.

Knowing exactly where she's going, Georgette turns the car off the street into a walled-off parking lot of what appears to be an old Spanish mission. "Welcome to Tiaquepaque!" she says as we roll to a stop.

This Spanish Mission, to my amusement, is actually shops and cafes. Stone floors surround three tier water fountains. Close-narrow paths to and from these shops create a quaint ambiance of romance. Georgette slips her arm around my waist. She apparently considers me her personal conquest. And I like it!

Shades of brown adobe open up to an open space, a plaza. A man is hard at work stretching cable and colored lights above and across a stage in the center of the plaza. An easel show card on a tripod reads Sedona Shakespeare Theater proudly presents "Taming of the Shrew."

Our gang of four chooses an out-of-the way cafe for its unique charm. With Italian flared checker tablecloths, the place has one major advantage. It offers outside dining with a panoramic and surrounding view of the red rock cliffs. This is the best place we could possibly be at this moment in our lives. Glass containers of solar herbal teas line the railing around the patio. When Georgette and I toast each other with tinkling ice filled tea glasses, our eyes lock. Instantly we both know where and how this day must end.

Chapter Nineteen

A midafternoon sun combines with a cool Flagstaff mountain breeze that graces through windows of my fourth-floor corner penthouse suite of the Monte Vista Hotel.

Georgette slinks across the ledge of the open window. Her catlike body leans over the sill to watch the hustle and bustle of the citizenry and tourists below. As she turns to smile at me, we know no words need to be spoken.

She pulls off her shirt to reveal a gold blouse, mysteriously unbuttoned. Her breasts are caressed in place by a sheer brassiere. I hold out her right arm to start nibbling her fingertips down to her palm. My lips then slowly trace back toward her inside elbow. She giggles at my touch before closing her eyes. Her head leans backward. With hot breath, I dart my tongue ever so lightly around her earlobe, purposely moving slower, causing her to breathe heavier. She's now fully at ease. Her blouse slips off one shoulder, then the other as it falls to the floor. Leaning back comfortably into the wide sill of the push up window; she grasps at my shoulders. "Mmmm, so muscular . . ." she murmurs, pulling me closer.

I adore how her long-reddish hair flows out the window, I nibble at her cleavage. Her sighs warm my loins and I harden. She moans as her youthful legs wrap around my waist. I want her and . . . I know that she wants me. But . . . not yet.

Her fingertips firmly run down my spine, and in one experienced, single motion, pulls off my shirt. Instantly those same fingers grip and run over my chest. As her palms rest over my hairy pecs, she squeezes her legs tighter.

I pull her to me, my lips nibble more firmly in and about her inviting throat. My thumbs caress her breasts. Her breathing becomes heavier.

"Take it off," she demands.

With a quick snap, my hands free the garment hook. Another piece of her clothing falls freely revealing supple breasts.

"Oh, they are so lovely," I whisper to her. She pulls my head to her chest, guiding my lips to each hard tip. My tongue lightly darts and tastes around the nipple, carefully avoiding its center. This only seems to make her breathe more heavily. "I want you."

I stare into her eyes and grin. "Oh, no, no. You are not ready for me yet," I whisper. My hands cradle her breasts, teasing the firm, hard nipples between my fingers. I want her to crave me much more.

Her fingernails massage my scalp then run down my back, gripping along the way. My fingertips slowly but firmly massage the base of her skull down each notch of her spine. I pay close attention to each notch down to her hips as I kiss her swollen breasts. My hands move under her skirt, cradling her firm bottom.

"Do you like what you're holding?" she whispers while nibbling my ear lobe.

"I love how you feel in my hands," I whisper back. Like a magician pulling the tablecloth from under a fully laid out table, I pull her skirt off along with her panties. More garments fall to the carpet.

I take a few steps back wanting to see her beauty before me. Bringing in her folded legs to her chest, she sits on the windowsill to catch the warmth of the setting sun. As orange glow reflects through the window and into my eyes, I study her seductive silhouette. Oh, I want her. But not yet.

As my eyes caress her, she appears simply angelic. I cradle her right ankle in one hand and begin massaging her little toe. Then, on to the next and the next till I work up the foot with a firm grip. Then her left foot receives my touch. All along my eyes savor the view.

"You like doing that, don't you?" she asks.

"I definitely love rolling my hands all over every inch of your beautiful body, woman!" I can hear my own passion ripping through my voice.

She immediately wraps her legs around my waist again. Placing her arms around my shoulders, she pulls herself up to me. I lift her out of the windowsill, carry her a few steps away to the king size, four poster brass bed.

Just as I stare into her eyes, the phone rings its bicycle bell sound.

"I'm hearing bells baby," I tell her.

The time has come, so I choose to ignore the phone. I'm going to take her. I reach for her as the phone rings again. Its constant chiming drains my passions.

She moans with frustration. "Ignore it."

"Ah babe. I'm trying," I say nibbling at her breasts. The bicycle bells ring echoes louder.

"Darling, if I don't answer, it won't stop. I'll make it real quick."

Reluctantly, she releases her leg embrace. With only sweat to cover me, I cross the room and grab the receiver.

"What? Um, Hello!" I demand. Not bothering to hide my frustration, "Who is it?"

"Hello?" came a distant male voice. "Ronn? Ronn how's it going?" It's apparent this voice is expecting to be recognized.

Still in a euphoric haze, I ask, "Yeah. Yeah. Who is this?"

"It's Lee. Lee Parks. I'm calling from Seattle. Returning your call. You left a message to call you at this number!"

Damn it! He's right. "Yeah. Lee! Lee Parks! Yeah, how've you been man? Long time no talk."

"Ever since I moved up here, life's been active. I've been doing plenty of shows. And most important, I've gotten engaged. Life's been pretty good."

I focus on this call that I've been waiting on for a week. "I wanted to let you know that I got this new club down here in Flagstaff, Arizona. I want you to play here. You'd be a big hit because I haven't presented any magicians yet. You'd kill here, man." My eyes move from the phone's push buttons to my lovely naked prey stretched out only a few steps away. My attention slips between this important phone call and this youthful redhead beauty demanding my attention.

"I'd love to come down there, but I don't know when my schedule will allow me," Lee's long distance voice explains.

Georgette notices my phone dilemma. She slinks over to sit down in front of me on the carpet.

"We've got to see what we can do to get you booked to play this place. What can we do to make it happen?" I look down to her yearning eyes. My hand palms her cheek, then I run my fingers through her flowing red hair.

As if by instinct, her lips find their way. Not really expecting her eager action, my knees begin to buckle at the pleasure.

"Well it sounds like a trip I should make then, Ronn," Lee says. "What dates look good to you?"

Her motions build up my passion once again, clouding my mind, and sidetracking the conversation. "Ah, ah Lee, so do you want to play here?"

"I just said what dates look good to ya?"

Georgette giggles while running her tongue down each leg to the knee then back to command central. She enjoys the power.

"Georgette!" I grip the receiver harder while leaning against the wall. "Lee, I guess I need to look at the calendar book." My knees buckle. "Listen, Lee? Ah, um I'm having a hard time . . ."

She spits with laughter. "Hard time."

"Do you have a lady there?" Lee asks.

"Oh, yeah."

"No wonder I'm hearing what I'm hearing, you dirty dog. You should have told me. It sounded like she was jerking you off."

Embarrassed, I hope he was just kidding. "Well you know how it is? Business is business."

"Let me call you back at a better time. Like maybe when business isn't so, so sweaty. What do you say?"

"Well, thanks, my man. But we do have to talk soon and lock up some dates when I have my book handy."

"Yeah. Okay. And speaking about being handy, say hello to your Georgette for me," he laughs.

"Sir, that will be a great pleasure indeed and in more ways than one," I say. Her hot lips and tongue find my bare throat.

"Lee, Lee I need your phone number up there, Lee. Lee!" But all I hear is a dead phone on the other end. I leave the phone receiver dangling off the hook. It swings against the wall.

Chapter Twenty

Several weeks pass. Then on the Thursday prior to the usual Monty V. weekend, I am behind the wheel of Georgette's Beemer, again. Our two-lane highway winds north toward the Grand Canyon. Traffic is thick going both ways through pine tree forests that finally level off to open, thinned out shrubbery amidst a red dirt landscape. Georgette and I sit quietly beside each other, concentrating on our winding trek north.

Tonight, I will be the very first in the history of the world to produce a comedy club concert at the great American natural phenomenon, The Grand Canyon.

Georgette and I have been close during this time. Upon completion of each week's Flagstaff run, I return to Albuquerque. She stays in Flagstaff wrapping up her summertime college courses.

Tonight, the amphitheater on the rim will fill with smiles, giggles and laughs. The sun will sink below the horizon and we will have a majestic panoramic view as our backdrop. My show will be a couple of old Duke City Comedy Club All Stars. A former marine comic, Bill Thomas, will soon be stationed at Quantico in Virginia. And, of course, my personal favorite, William (Weely) Cordova. I get to be the humble MC/producer.

My eyes sidetrack to Georgette's tanned legs. It seems only natural for my right hand to caress her inner thigh. She says nothing as it seems my touch relaxes her even more.

Chapter Twenty-One

I'm on top of the world. My production career is bringing in steady and greater unique opportunities. Plus, I will be sharing this career high with a lovely lady. I am so happy to be with her during this once-in-a-lifetime event.

The two-way traffic is busy in both directions. As we wait, Georgette stretches out while my hands rest patiently on top of the steering wheel. Her hand seems to naturally stroll over to the nape of my neck, running the tips of her fingers through my hair. I feel complete.

I have become reliant on her. Part of me hates that. But it's being lonely that affects my thinking. Georgette has been mentioning with regularity that within weeks she'll be graduating with a BA in Education from NAU, which her parents paid for. They expect her back in Tucson in August to start an elementary school teaching job for the Tucson Public School System in September. Mom and Dad are doctorate honchos there. Her life is planned in granite.

But also, she tosses about the idea of marriage. She's so receptive to me that she feels free to suggest with extra emphasis that I move my headquarters to the cactus deserts of Tucson. I do not want to settle down in the conventional sense. Why? We've already been practicing the honeymoon. But can we live together? Or even worse, can we live without each other? This, I need to learn.

"We're at the entrance of the Grand Canyon National Park," I tell Georgette as we pull up under the portal of the Squire Inn Hotel. Only then does she pull her fingers from my hair.

"This little town has the Indian name of Tuceon, Arizona," she tells me.

I silently think of the name similarity of the Arizona city four hours south of here.

Georgette pushes the hotel room door open as I carry in our luggage. She follows and falls face first on the king size bed. "That ride took it out of me."

"I've got to clean up and get to the amphitheater for a light and sound tech rehearsal," I tell her. "You can have the room to prepare yourself, darling." I drop the luggage and swing my briefcase onto the phone desk.

"We can save some time and precious water if you'd like to shower together," she says.

I stop in my tracks, immediately forgetting my business arrangements, and step toward her. All I can do is let her pull me down to her breasts as she pulls off my shirt. Just then the phone rings. I ignore it, but it rings again. So, I have to answer.

"Ronn. You're here, good. It's Weely."

I can hear wild children screaming in the background. Weely Cordova brought his family. After all he is a family man, and this is the Grand Canyon.

"The most eminent lowrider comic is calling me. We just got in ourselves. How's it going? Are you in the hotel yet? Have you spoken to Bill yet?"

In the background Weely's five kids scream as Irene tries to control them. "Yeah, Bill and me just spoke, hold on. We checked in last night . . . just a minute . . . sweetheart, daddy's on the phone. Go ask your mother and tell your brother to get some clothes on. Ronn? We needed to get away from home sooner, once I heard the news."

"You got some grief?" I inquire.

"Haven't you heard?" I wait. "Heard? Heard what?" I hear silence. "You're scaring me man. Heard what?" Georgette listens in.

"Lee Parks had a heart attack. He died."

My butt falls on the closest chair. "What?!" My heart pounds.

"Bill told me. He flew to Seattle for his funeral. Apparently three or four weeks ago Lee was just walking down some staircase when he simply collapsed."

My mood catches with the news. "I just spoke with him." Then I realize it's been a month since we spoke in Flagstaff.

"The grapevine was slow getting to us. I'm told his fiancé had to arrange the funeral there in Seattle. I guess he didn't have any relatives."

"Yeah, he told me during our Chinatown days that he was an orphan. I talked to him about a month ago. It had to happen shortly thereafter." I was supposed to contact him too. But, because of this lady in my life, I got sidetracked. I simply forgot to follow up. It hits me now, why Lee didn't contact me either. Glancing at my lady sitting up to listen in, I remember what I was doing the last time I talked to Lee Parks. My gut begins to ache.

"Ronn . . . Ronn?" Weely voices up to me. "What do you want to do about tonight's show?"

"Bill and you are pros. We still have to do the show. There is no choice. We have to do it."

"I don't want to go on stage tonight," admits Weely. "But we don't have no choice, do we?"

"And compadre, no one can know any different, right?"

"Right," Weely agrees and we both hang up softly.

Chapter Twenty-Two

The orange-tinted Grand Canyon panorama is framed for the audience between two light posts focused toward the not-yet-lit amphitheater stage. Only minutes separate the audience from evening as the sun slowly sinks. Mother Nature now demonstrates her talent as a live performance artist and sculptor. Bright oranges, reds, and golden hues paint the sculpted abyss before us. But light quickly changes them into dark shades of greens, blues, purples, then into complete black. In this heartbeat of time, just before nightfall, the stage speakers emit deep base drum beats. The stage lights snap on to cover the empty stage.

I had an opportune moment to change the pre-show music from the previously planned, light-hearted musical intro which no one in the show was in the mood to hear. So, I changed it to trumpets blare out as if to announce to the world of the coming. Opening passages from America's composer Aaron Copeland's "Fanfare to the Common Man" set the mood.

I open the show with a microphone from backstage.

"And now, ladies and gentlemen, bowing to the beauty of Mother Nature, we are extremely proud to announce a night filled with smiles, giggles and laughs!" I keep in beat with the pulsating drums. "The time has arrived to kick back and loosen up. Stretch out ladies and gentlemen, so your ribs will not be sore from laughter after this comedy experience!" Trumpets underscore my words. "Please, with a healthy round of applause, bring to the stage your MC and producer of the Route Sixty-Six Comedy Club . . . Ronn . . . Greco!" I finish the unusual task of introducing myself as the music fades away. I hand the mic to a stage-hand and smile. I walk onto the lit stage under a round of strong applause.

At the microphone stand, stage center, I take a bow. "Ladies and gentlemen, I bow to the greatest opening performer in the world: Mother Nature. Please, let's give her a round of applause."

Raising my hand and turning my back on the audience to look out over the canyon and whisper, "We're dedicating this show to you, buddy." I bow to almighty supremacy. I turn back to face my audience. "As your comedy producer, Ronn Greco, I am happy to attempt to match that tonight! How are you Ladies and Gentlemen?"

Applause fades. I look out beyond the lights to see tiers of smiling and anticipating faces. Theatrical senses kick in, pushing everything else in my mind aside.

"Good Evening. The Route Sixty-Six Comedy Club will provide you some kicks tonight. As your producer and MC, I am proud to present a fine array of national comedy talent on this stage. Soon, you'll see your comedy headliner. He's a fellow who just wrapped up his tour as a United States Marine sergeant, where he toured every American military base around the world with the USO. He has performed miles above ground in Air Force One, as well as miles below the sea for sailors in a Nuclear Trident Submarine. After his performance here tonight, he goes to Quantico in Virginia, where he begins a new comedy career. He'll be shooting his own TV pilot for the new national comedy cable TM network, Comedy Central. I remember when he started his career on my stage five years ago. I'm so proud of him. Bill Thomas is here tonight!" Applause rings out.

"But before you see him, you'll see another of my personal favorite comics. If you don't know what a lowrider comic is, you will after this show. National up-and-coming comic sensation, William Weely Cordova, will be on this spot tonight." Another round of applause rises and lowers. "But up front, ladies and gentlemen, if I may introduce your MC. That's me. How do you do?"

117

The audience's smiles grow even wider in anticipation.

Chapter Twenty-Three

It's time to talk about our future together. In a week, Mommy and Daddy are expecting her back in Tucson to start her new job at Poke Elementary School. And, to my chagrin, I only recently learned that she still hasn't even told them about me. Thereby the reason for this trip together.

From Flagstaff, south thru Phoenix, we drive into Tucson to meet the parents. And with the way it's turning out, I'm seeing that Georgette has different thoughts.

Arriving in Tucson, I want to check into a motel so I can freshen up. But no. She wants to go straight to the school where Mom is preparing for her new season of classes. I shouldn't have to expect this very important initial meeting to happen yet.

"I haven't had a chance to shower, shave or dress. After the very long and hot drive, I'm not ready," I tell her.

Georgette just smiles. I figure I have no options because she's bringing her mother out to meet me as I find myself standing in the middle of her mom's empty high school classroom.

Georgette shows no emotion, "Hello mother."

A short and stout woman with closely cropped brown hair bolts from behind her desk. "Georgette! Georgette! This is a surprise!" Then a flurry of joyful incoherent noises ensue between mother and daughter.

Holding her mother warmly, she turns to me. "Mom, I want to introduce my fiancé, Ronn Greco."

Embarrassed, my grubby appearance makes me extremely self-conscious, having learned long ago the value of first impressions. "It's great to meet you," I say, while holding out my hand. "Please forgive my appearance, we're just off the road. I had hoped to freshen up before meeting you." I glance at Georgette. "May I suggest we leave you now and I will buy us all dinner tonight so we can get to know each other? I want to provide answers to the plethora of questions you must have."

***

After a fine dinner at Mr. and Mrs. Collin's favorite Italian restaurant, the surprise hits. Sitting around the table with empty plates in front of us, and a rainbow of colors reflecting from the beautiful crystal chandelier hanging over us, a truer picture develops.

These parents are an obvious loving couple. A grey haired, motherly matron and her distinguished husband show love for their only daughter. Yet it is apparent that they are being tested needlessly. Georgette cannot hide a flare for rebellion and seems grumpy that I am able to hold my own against the barrage of parental questions. I'm proving that I would be a loving and responsible man who would take care of their baby. I can tell she's used to bringing home boys, not a man.

Mr. Collins leans forward. "So Ronn, tell me more about this comedy club business of yours."

"My comedy club road company is working steady every week." I knock three times on the wooden table. "Here in Arizona, there's Flagstaff, Yuma and Springville. In Texas, there's El Paso and Lubbock. My New Mexico circuit consists of Las Cruces, Santa Fe and Farmington." I carefully leave out Albuquerque. "And right across the state border in Colorado, Durango. Albuquerque is the comfortable hub of all this weekly activity. Plus soon, the new casino town of Laughlin, Nevada will be coming on line."

Georgette then says, "I am strongly suggesting he relocate his headquarters from New Mexico to Tucson."

I interject, "But this is despite the fact I'm conveniently located only a block and a half away from Interstate Forty/old Route 66. This is the geometrical center of Albuquerque which is geometric center of New Mexico which is geometric center of the Route Sixty-Six Comedy Club Road Company circuit!"

Georgette says, "But, Mom and Dad, I am still working on him to change his mind. I know he and I can find a place together in Tucson. I've even offered to support him until he reestablishes his business."

I quickly insert, "It's a loving offer, and I'm grateful. But no twenty-two-year-old supports Ronn Greco."

I just confirmed to her parents that I'd take care of their daughter. Besides, one business fact remains. I'm not sure of the commercial viability of operating out of the southwestern coffin corner of my circuit.

The next day is a free Monday. We find time to meet some of her hometown friends while crashing at her girlfriend's apartment. And with this clear and warm Tucson night upon me, my plan is to sleep outside by the pool.

It's about three a.m. when she joins me. Shortly thereafter, I'm wondering if any of the apartment neighbors are hearing strange noises emitting from outside. But with a smile, and her taking me, why should I care?

A few hours later, we are traveling eastward in my new Mercury Zephyr to Las Cruces, New Mexico for my weekly Tuesday night show at the Hilton. We cruise over the blistering, sun bleached southern Arizona desert where only the meanest rattle snakes dare to roam. Occasional road signs invite travelers to visit Mexico only an hour south. Infrequent and sparse shrubbery dot the landscape. Rocky plateaus rise in the distance.

The windows are fully rolled down. Because of the morning air, we don't yet need air conditioning. She reclines back in the passenger seat. I rest my right hand over her inviting thigh. She seems to find this securing while proving to be our usual car riding position. With contented smiles, we roll eastward without a word between us. Her bare thigh sweats under my palm. But she says nothing. So, my hand smoothly moves closer to her warming crotch, massaging along the way. She simply responds by relaxing and spreading her tan legs farther apart. I glance over to her for approval, her eyes are closed under her sunglasses. Finally, my fingers dip under her shorts to feel moistness. She moans. I enjoy massaging with one hand while I steer eastward through southern Arizona with the other.

Her moans indicate she wants more. She adjusts by projecting her right leg out of the window, directing warmer air into the car.

"I want you. I want you now!" she teases.

Before I can say anything, an 18-wheeler pulls up in the lane beside us. Its cab looms over my Zephyr. A sudden roar of its engines along with the truck's trumpet horns blare. She jolts into an upright position, pulling in her outstretched leg.

"Oh, hell," she shouts. Her embarrassment is quick, and she flips the driver a finger.

I press the brakes to allow the truck to speed on. The trucker sticks his arm outside his window giving me a thumbs up. I cannot help but smile.

"You macho sonofabitch!" Georgette shouts at me as she slugs my shoulder.

I laugh. "I love you back . . ."

Suddenly and bluntly, the car hits a series of hard, pronounced thumps in the road. Ominously, they repeat. Jolts begin to drag and strongly force the Mercury Zephyr to the side of the road.

"Oh, my God! Oh, my God!" Georgette shrieks.

Déjà vu overwhelms me. Her shrieks next to me in the car sends me back five years. Am I going to kill her . . . again? Hell, no. I pull the car over to the shoulder and stop. This isn't the first blowout I've had in working over a hundred thousand miles in the last five years. And it probably won't be the last. Goes with the territory, I suppose.

Georgette loses it. "What are we going to do? What are we going to do?"

"No need to fret, baby. I'll take care of it." My gut relaxes as I get out to take a look. "Just as I thought." I look at the flattened rubber draping over gravel and pavement.

She jumps out of the car and sees that it is resting on the tire rim. "What are we going to do? What are we going to do?"

"Do you always repeat your questions when you're freaked?" I put my arms around her to embrace her shivering but sweaty body.

"Don't worry. I'll just change the flat with the spare. No big deal." Instantly, I feel her relax. With a quick kiss I release her.

I just pull off my shirt and immediately feel Georgette's eyes on me. Her tongue runs over her parched lips. I take out a blanket and toss it over my shoulder. My arm muscles ripple with sweat as I pull out the spare. I'm feeling the growing desert heat.

"If it wasn't so damn hot under this sun, I'd take you right here," Georgette says.

Black suet now covers my chest and arms when I finish the job. But I don't care. Obviously, she doesn't either. With the blanket over my shoulder, she's let me lead her into the desert. Arizona has been very good to me.

Chapter Twenty-Four

After checking into my usual 10th floor penthouse suite of the Las Cruces Hilton, the first thing I do is walk across the room to gander over the city from the western balcony.

"Come. Look." I take Georgette in my arms and we bathe in the fiery red and orange glare of the setting sun reflecting their colors throughout the hotel suite.

But, first things first. I step straight to the telephone. I dial a series of numbers to retrieve my phone messages. "Damn!" I want to shout out stronger language, but Georgette is in the room. She's learned to avoid saying anything during my outbursts.

"That . . ." I bite my tongue. ". . . that . . . that S.O.B. headliner out of L.A. backed out of this weekend's gigs for some off-the-wall reason. Who am I going to replace him with at the last minute? Especially from here? I need to be at my desk."

Immediately she knows, that without a word being said, our planned romantic dinner is suddenly and with great disappointment, canceled. But she understands. This is the nature of having a comedy producer for a fiancé.

When I break out my day planner/phone book to start making long distance, trouble-shooting phone calls, there isn't even a whimper from her.

An hour before showtime, I have a reason to be proud of myself. With only a few phone calls out of my handy dandy talent roster, my last minute replacement headliner dilemma is solved with just enough time for a quick shower before showtime. The problem is, Georgette has beaten me to the hot, well lit, steam filled room.

As I walk into the room to see her opaque image through the shower door, she says, "This hot water feels oh so good all over my body. Especially after the long, long day."

I open the shower door and step in. The only thing between her pink skin and my hairy, Arizona tanned body is the hotel-provided shampoo.

Chapter Twenty-Five

The show is a success, which is no surprise to me. Because of the adrenaline rush and emotional high that I feel, all I want to do is take my sweet young thing back upstairs. But first, while she dances her little heart away to the DJ's multi-colored, laser-lit, pulsating showroom, I need to meet with the GM to plan the next schedule of shows, collect my pay for tonight and disperse the green to my comic troopers.

On my way upstairs, I glance into the showroom. Disco lights, in sync with the dance beat, flash into my eyes. There she is, swaying her pulsating body in unison with the others in a line dance. After the long day, dancing is the last thing on my mind. I go upstairs to wait for her.

Soon this college girl will get her fill of the electric buzz of the dance floor. I know she'll want to be satisfied in other ways as well. And with the long day I've had, those other ways will require all the energy my thirty-eight-year-old body can produce.

Chapter Twenty-Six

The next morning, we head north on Interstate 25 to Albuquerque. The route is as familiar as, like the cliché says, the back of my hand. I'm reenergized while Georgette's curled up in an embryonic state in the passenger seat, napping. I smile.

I was the totally drained one while she wanted more. Now, she's the one drained. Last night was the first time I had ever been tied up in bed from wrists to ankles. Where does she get all of these ideas?

It's great to get home. Pulling into the driveway, I see Dad sitting on his lawn chair, obviously happy to see me pull in. It's as if he knew when I'd be getting home.

"Wake up darling. I want you to meet my father." She instantly blossoms and wipes the sleep from her eyes. "We'll rest a couple of hours. I've got about an hour of work ahead at my desk. The week's books have to get done, that kind of thing. But first, Dad would love to meet a lovely lady."

I step out of my comedy Conestoga wagon and greet Dad with a bear hug. "How's it going, Pop? It's good to be home. This was a great road trip and I have someone I want you to meet." I lead my old man toward the Zephyr. "I've told you about her . . ."

Not wanting to wait, Georgette gets out and greets my father. "I like your father, he's so cute. Just like you," she says to me. She shakes Dad's hand. "It's a real pleasure Sir, to meet you."

Feeling frisky, she pinches my rear as I lead them in the front door. We walk to the rear of the house and under a doorway to the nerve center of the Route Sixty-Six Comedy Club Road Company. The sight immediately intrigues her. Every square foot of wall space is covered with show posters, comedian photos, road maps and a wall schedule layout. The entire ceiling is plastered with movie posters. A six-foot-long desk stretches out from the corner. A typewriter anchors the side. On the opposite side of the room, a TV and VCR hookup are sandwiched between multiple stacks of videos.

I swing open the door in the far corner of the office. Fresh air waves over us from the outside.

"This is normally the main entrance," I say.

"It would be a long time before I got bored in here," Georgette says. "So much to see." She looks at each item in turn.

Taking it for granted, I toss my gear on the floor and the briefcase on the desk.

"We'll take it easy for a couple of hours, then pick up my headliner, Jake the ventriloquist, at six o'clock. They'll enjoy him in Flagstaff."

Sitting at my desk, I push the answering machine buttons. She says nothing, smiling as she watches me do my thing in my environment. She stretches out on the couch across the office from my desk while following my practiced routine of pulling out files, while cross-checking calendars. The phone rings.

"Greetings! Ronn Greco here." I spin around in my chair to gander at the seductive young thing stretched out on the couch. "Hey Jason! How's it going in Hollywood?"

Georgette watches me.

"You can't be in New Mexico?" I just listen. "Hey that's great! When do you have to show up on the set?" Damn! This is another cancellation, I deduce. "Yeah that's right. That's the week you're booked with me, September 15 thru 20," I confirm. "Well that's great for you, congrats! When these flicks' casting calls, you got to jump on the bandwagon." I cover the receiver before silently cussing under my breath. "Well, when new dates are available, I'll call," when hell freezes over, I think. "Take it easy. And again, congratulations." I firmly place down the receiver. "Damn it! I hate cancellations!" I'm talking more to myself than to my guest. "Two in one week!"

"What's wrong, darling?"

"A headliner I had coming in three weeks just canceled. He's a Hollywood actor and apparently he just got a part in a Western being shot up in Santa Fe the week I had him booked. Damn. But how can I argue with a movie part?" I laugh!

"The only good thing was that I was paying him three times more than his comic talent was worth. I was just paying him for his TV credentials." He can see her interest peak. "You would recognize him if you saw him because of that TV sitcom he was in when you were barely a teenager," I suddenly smile at the tease. But my agitated mind quickly returns. "He would draw an audience only because of his recognition factor. And not for his comic ability, that's for sure."

"Out of curiosity, how much were you paying him?"

"Seven shows, fifteen hundred bucks." I looked her straight in the eyes. "These cancellations are killing me." I massage my stressed facial muscles. The whiskers rubbing against my palms remind me of my five o'clock shadow.

Georgette bounces over as I fumble at my desk with muffled frustration. Expertly, her hands begin to knead my rigid neck muscles. She works across my shoulders, then down my spine, I melt.

Again, the phone rings, snapping me back to reality. She pushes my outreached hand away to answer the phone herself.

"Good afternoon. The Route Sixty-Six Comedy Club Road Company," she says. "Yes, and who is calling please? I will see if he's in. Please hold." She places her hand over the receiver.

"Hey, you're good," I say.

"Anything for you, baby," she smiles.

"It's a Peter Conrad, calling from New York. Are you in?"

"It's Petrof! Sure." I take the receiver. "Hey, Petrof, what the heck are you, a Wisconsin boy, doing in New York?"

"Hey Buddy, how are you? I'm glad I caught you in," he says. "I'm talking to editors and agents. Trying to get something going with my novel."

"You've got great timing, we just got in thirty minutes ago!"

"Fantastic, fantastic. That's a good omen. Listen, Buddy, I'm in a jam. I'm trying to work my way back to Arizona. I've got some work out there in late September, and I just had some fall outs in Texas. Got anything in mid-September?"

I place my hand over the receiver and say to Georgette, "I think the Lord is smiling on both of us." So I tell Petrof, "I just had a fall out for those same dates of September 15 through 20 in Arizona. How are those dates for you?"

"Arizona? Perfect! Fantastic! Ink me in. What's the pay?"

"Seven shows . . .? Listen I'm over stressed on that week. I could barely afford what I thought I could pay. You'll be returning the favor if you could do it for five hundred."

He hesitates. "Can you do a little better than that, like with an airline ticket, maybe that way I can come out ahead?"

"Of course, that's fair. Buy it and I will refund it to you."

"You got me! Ink me in. Thanks a lot man. You are a lifesaver. I'll pick up a ticket tomorrow and we'll talk the week before on the agenda. And thanks. Talk to you soon."

"Hold your horses, Petrof. I'll need the usual promo material sent to me like yesterday. I don't think I have any more of your stuff on file. Send it immediately. And Petrof, thank you. You helped me, too." Both of us hang up with relief. I shoot up out of my desk chair. "Can you believe that? It's seldom that easy! Plus, I saved half of what I was going to spend before in the process!" I turn to Georgette. "That's bucks that will eventually go to a certain wedding." My voice trails off.

She is stretched out on the couch across the room. Her blouse is removed, highlighting a black bra. Her unbuttoned short shorts reveal a hint of her black panties. She stretches her arms toward me. As if I had no will of my own, I step toward her. In no time, my hand sweeps under her panties to cradle her buttocks while my tongue and lips graze over her breast. She instantly wraps her arms around me.

Six hours later, I'm saying my weekly goodbyes to Dad. I see a certain sadness in his eyes but have no time to ask why. With effort, I force it out of my mind.

Georgette shakes his hand. "Again, sir, I must say it was a pleasure meeting you." She continues to wave as he stands on the lawn watching us drive down the street and around the corner toward Interstate Forty.

In no time at all, the Mercury Zephyr is on the road with a third party, the comedian/ventriloquist Jason Pierson. As we head west toward Flagstaff, Arizona, our plan is the same even though we left Albuquerque later than planned.

After five hours of seventy-five miles an hour, nighttime driving, we're all exhausted. So, when our midnight arrival at the Monte Vista Hotel does happen, the sparkling excitement of our arrival is gone. The travel time has gripped all of our bones. All three of us just want to go to bed. After all, Georgette and I have to get up early in the morning. We have our first sexless night in some time.

We leave for the road to Tucson the next morning. But first Georgette has to pick up her last college records. So, now I wait in the car outside NAU's registrar's office. I watch college kids walk the campus or ride their bicycles to and fro, when it hits me. Georgette is not much different in age than these kids! I instantly feel out of place, which brings another realization. I'm Georgette's last college fling! She has told me that many times in her own way. She's finished with school and is happy to get out. It fits. I am her last fling.

She senses something's bothering me as we drive to her girlfriend's apartment. We're both silent when she asks, "What's on your mind, baby?"

I can't hold back any longer. "Am I your last college fling? Will there be a future for us once I drop you off and return to my world?"

"That's silly. Put those thoughts out of your mind, especially today. I don't want to make this temporary separation more difficult than it already is. Do you?"

She sounds wise for her years, yet I still detect a certain lack of conviction in her voice. On the other hand, she is right about making this harder. So, when we're a few blocks from our destination, my decision is easy. I want to be sure of her. We pull into the parking lot of her girlfriend's apartment.

"Because of your new schedule and my circuit commitments," I say, "Let's stay in contact over the next several weeks by phone."

"I can come up on weekends to meet you in Flagstaff," she offers.

"That would be great, but it's not realistic, sweetheart. Face it, you have to get acclimated to your new teaching job and settled in your new apartment. We'll stay as close as possible till we can get together. We're only a phone call away." Even I don't believe in my meager attempt to test the durability of this relationship.

Chapter Twenty-Seven

At the end of this almost two-thousand-mile trip, we both know that we have to make a decision.

Despite the 100 degree temperatures of Tucson, she trembles in my arms as we stand beside the hot metal of the car, saying our goodbyes. There is no hesitation as our lips meet.

In driving away, back the three hours to Flagstaff, my chest falls at the sight of her crying eyes. I want to stop and turn around, but the feeling of being nothing more than a fling still gnaws at my gut. A little time apart will test our resolve. After all, we haven't been apart for more than three days since we met.

The first week brings a phone call every night. She is starting teaching and must get up by 5:30 each morning. She said that she doesn't like going to bed so early. By the second week, I find it's more challenging to match her schedule with mine. Catching her at home when I call has been difficult. Three out of seven nights is all I manage to call. And by the third week, only one call per week is making contact. Finally, the last conversation we had was very cold and abrupt.

After a month I feel the need to see her right away. Without bothering to notify her that I'm coming, I leave Flagstaff early one Sunday morning to drive to Tucson. I'll surprise her by going straight to the apartment where I dropped her off only a month ago.

I schlep across five hours of desert to that apartment to knock on the door. But no one answers. I look through the window, the place is empty. When I ask the manager, he says, "They just moved out last week. The nervous red head said they didn't have a forwarding address yet."

This 4th floor Hilton Hotel room was to host another romantic interlude, or so I had hoped. Instead, I leave a batch of phone calls on her answering machine. Yet, no response.

The evening brings a thunderous rainstorm. Which has to be rare for Tucson. Giant lightning displays fill the sky that seem to project a giant television-like image across the wall-sized window into my darkened room. The variety of miniature liquors in the mini refrigerator keep me company. The room's sofa chair allows me to watch an entertainment production provided by the best entertainment producer there is, Mother Nature.

From my 4th floor view, framed by open curtains, crackling then booming thunder vibrates the walls, providing my surround sound. Each bolt of lightning brings another swig of whiskey, bourbon, or rum. Thunder brings two swigs. By the time the liquid concession stand is empty, I don't even want to keep my eyelids open.

Clouds have blown away, revealing a full moon and bright stars by the time the phone finally rings. By the fourth ring, my senses kick in and I fly across the room to grab the receiver. The clock radio beside the phone flashes 3:30 am.

A stern, monotone teacher's voice comes from the other end. "Ronn? This is Georgette."

"Darling, I've been trying to reach you. I've called everywhere. I'm in town to see you." I wipe the sleep from my eyes through a groggy brain.

"Well, I can't see you. Now is not a good time."

"Not now at 3:30 in the morning, of course. But let's say, over breakfast here at the hotel?"

"This is not easy for me. And you're making it more difficult . . . we shouldn't see each other anymore." Her voice remains matter of fact.

It's a moment before I can speak again. "But Georgette? I came to see you."

"You were right about you being my last college fling. You live a different life than I do now. I should hang up here before I say something that I shouldn't." A tinge of emotion squeaks into her voice.

A realization hits me. "Well, babe, if that's how you want it? That's how you want it." I am hurt, "I'm not going to argue with you." I wait for her to say something, but all I hear is a practiced silence, so I have to say something. "It was great while it lasted. And if you want it to end this way, remember that it was your call. I will oblige you." Again, I remain silent, hoping that she'll say something positive. "I'll hang up now because you've said what you've obviously been planning." I immediately hope that she'll say something to stop me. But she remains quiet. "Well, darling, your silence says more than words could."

"It's over between us. Let's end it here," she simply says.

"Do I deserve a reason? Or am I as disposable as you make it sound? We haven't spoken in more than a week."

"Listen to me. Go live your life and I'll live mine," she snaps.

Stalling, stalling, I don't want to hang up. "What is there left to say? I came to town because I needed to see you, but you are obviously no longer interested in what we had." She continues her ice-cold silence. "If you refuse to even talk to me, I guess this has to be it. I wish you the best." Again, she says nothing. "All right . . . good-bye!" I slam down the receiver.

This always happens when you get involved with groupies. Why am I so surprised? The room gets darker as I grieve back to sleep.

Chapter Twenty-Eight

A month later, the Monte Vista Hotel has grown into just another drab and dreaded gig. I drove through New Mexico and Arizona to get here from last night's gig in El Paso, Texas, to find a phone message waiting. Georgette wants me to call her in Tucson. She's the last person I expected to hear from.

Up in my room, I stare at the slip of paper with her number on it. Do I call now? I have a show to do in less than an hour and I still have to shower and get focused. I place the slip of paper on the nightstand and head to the bathroom. The shirt comes off as I walk there, but its only moments later that I find myself pushing the buttons on the wall phone. As I prepare to talk into the old fashioned phone, I look forward to talking with her.

But I don't recognize the strange foreign accented male voice that answers. "Hello, hello!"

"Hello? Excuse me. I don't know if I got the right number. Is Georgette Collins in?"

"Yeah, yeah. Who is this?" snaps the foreign accent.

"Ronn Greco calling from Flagstaff returning a phone message."

The voice shouts out from the other end. "Georgette, phone! Long Distance. Make it quick." I can hear the receiver being handed to her. "Make it quick," orders the foreign accent again.

"Hello, Ronn?"

"Georgette? How are you, gal?"

"Ah, good, it's you. I got to talk to you, hold on a minute." I can hear her tell the guy to hang up the extension. "Hello again, Ronn."

"Hi baby, how have you been?"

"I've been getting my life back in order."

"Was it all messed up or something? Is your new job getting you into the 8 to 5 mode?"

She ignores my question. "I did not call to converse. I've got to get to the point here, and it's not easy," she says.

"Still living in the same apartment?" I ask without letting her talk. "Your roommate there must be helping out on your expenses?"

She takes a deep breath, "Ronn, Haman is not my roommate. He's my fiancé," she says. "We're living together."

My gut tightens, "Congratulations," I mumble. "I guess that's why you wanted to break up with me. I should have known." I'm unable to hide my disappointment.

"No and yes, I guess. It's because of Haman that I'm calling you. When he asked me to marry him, I immediately said yes."

I'm unable to speak.

She continues, "And that's why I have to talk to you. Haman insists it's necessary to clear the air because of the guilt I feel. I've told him everything about you and me. He is to be my husband after all. And my new Muslim faith requires a cleansing of the soul."

"Muslim? Holy Jesus! What does the Muslim faith have to do with this?"

"He's from Lebanon and I've agreed to convert to his faith."

My gut churns even more at the thought of how quickly she's made life changing decisions in the months since we last saw each other. "So, what's this to me? You once told me that you didn't want to convert to Catholicism." I am close to losing control. "Is that why you're feeling guilty?"

She stays calm. "I can understand your feelings. Haman said you would naturally feel this way. But Ronn, you must have realized that I am the type of woman who needs her man around her. You are always traveling. I need my man with me. When you and I were apart, I realized that you would always be gone more than you'd be home . . . Ronn, I got pregnant by you."

My stomach contracts. "What? Why didn't you tell me? Why now? When are you due?"

"Ronn. Ronn. I knew it couldn't work between us. I didn't want to tell you because I knew how you'd respond. Some sort of knee jerk reaction would have caused you to feel guilty into marrying me. But it never would work. So, I had an abortion."

My jaw drops.

"That's why I couldn't see you that night you came to Tucson," she continues. "I just had it and didn't want to face you."

I grip the phone with all my strength. "I don't know what to say to you," I admit through my anger.

"Haman feels it's necessary for you to know, so he and I can proceed. He'll take care of me. He's a millionaire, and I do not want to lose him. I need him. Please try to understand. I wish you all my best in your life. Ronn, good-bye." She hangs up.

I slam the phone into its wall hook. "That bitch! Bitch!" If there ever is the worst crime between a man and woman, she committed it. I punch the wall, pounding it over and over again. "Turn the knife harder, you damn bitch," I shout and don't care who hears.

The familiar tone of telephone bicycle bell chimes fills the room, commanding me to answer the phone. I stare at it with rage, just let it ring till it stops. But it starts ringing again. On the fourth ring, I have to answer. "Yeah!"

"Ronn? All right, I'm glad that you're finally in. This is Jenny down in the showroom. That radio DJ from KNAU who says he was to MC tonight says he can't make it in. But he'll be in tomorrow. I knew you needed to know. Does that mean that you'll have to MC? Ronn. Ronn? Did you hear me?"

My inner mind orders me to calm down. Now! "Yeah, yeah. I'll be right down after I shower." I must compose myself immediately, "And Jenny, thanks." I tense at the emotional strain of having to control myself.

I focus on the water shooting down onto my face, forcing the stress and my tears away. I have to go out and be funny despite my knotted gut. I just want to put my fist through the face of that Haman guy. Helplessness is all I feel. But right now, I have no choice. I have to go on stage in a few minutes and maintain myself in front of hundreds of eyeballs. I have to force myself to think and focus on my tried and proven act.

But as the shower water eases the stress, all I can think of is one simple fact. For a short time there, I was going to be a father.

Chapter Twenty-Nine

The oldest veteran

Patriotism fills the 1991 American air. The red, white and blue proudly waves everywhere, and American troops are on the move. The news media constantly report they are going to face the most horrible killing fields since WWI. Other voices state it's nothing more than obvious media hype. Nevertheless, everyone wants to support our troops.

All my shows are the same in the Southwestern small towns on my comedy circuit, but more men and women are in uniform in the audiences. And many shows are becoming going away parties for those shipping out.

I now present benefit comedy shows at Albuquerque's Veteran's Hospital whenever I'm in town. I like to think I'm putting on my own USO show.

Last night's January snowstorm wasn't obliging, I can see. I patiently wait for my main attraction as I stand outside the Spanish Mission hospital canteen watching the silent grace of the falling snow picture in front of me.

Finally, my eyes catch a lone automobile, a white 1991 Cadillac passing through the far-off grounds gate. It's a float of snow passing by multiple flag poles that line the approaching path. The only colors are the multiple red, white and blue waving proudly. Weaving closer, I can now see gold trimmed hub caps. My mentor has arrived.

The motivation and guidance I've needed over the years to evolve into an entertainment producer has come from Frank Crosby. He is called Mr. Terrific. Not because he's so great, but because if something is great, he says, "Terrific!" And if things are not great, he says, "Terrific!"

Frank moved to Albuquerque right after WWII. He used to be a pro comedian himself in the closing days of Vaudeville, prior to the Great War. As far as I'm concerned, Frank Crosby is my elder statesman of the entertainment production business.

With my hand already out to shake, I smile and greet Frank. "This is a terrific day to go on stage isn't it, Frank?"

"Terrific!" he says in his high-pitched voice. Years ago, long before I met him, Frank survived throat cancer. The successful operation left his throat partially intact, with a high pitched, squeaky, speaking voice.

"I tried watching that Improv show on TV last night," he says. "But those young comics weren't so good. There weren't any good jokes I could steal."

We walk side by side inside and are greeted full blast by the heat. Frank's six-foot, two inch frame towers over me. He is impeccable in a pink suit, a color that matches his complexion, which is topped by his thinning white hair. He carries himself straight and erect. The ten laps he does daily in his pool serve him well. I think that I'd like to be as healthy as Frank when I'm his age.

Three on each side, ten-foot long, colored plaques from the various military services adorn the walls. Viga ceiling beams cross overhead from the entrance to the stage on the far end. Video machines, ping pong and pool tables are pushed to the side of the gymnasium's huge room to make way for rows and rows of folding chairs.

"They all smell the same, these hospital memories," Frank says.

Military patients, some in hospital gowns and coats, roll in on wheelchairs, pushed by their nurses. Others stand on crutches. All wait for the show to start as the area slowly fills up, chair by chair with past and present members of the American Armed Forces.

Backstage, I begin to psych myself up along with my two comics and a magician.

The hospital administrator walks apprehensively onto the stage and slowly approaches the lone microphone.

"Now, ladies and gentlemen, it is a beautiful day to bring some laughter into our lives." His voice drones on. "We are very lucky to have a group of comic entertainers from the Route Sixty-Six Comedy Club visiting with us today. So, are you ready?" The audience is half inspired. "Now, let me introduce your MC and producer of the show, Ronn Greco!"

I enter the stage with a giant smile. Shaking the administrator's hand with both of mine, I reach for the microphone.

"Good afternoon, ladies and gentlemen! It's more than an honor to bring my gang of laugh meisters here to smile, giggle and laugh with you. Also, hopefully to make a couple of things disappear." Suddenly I feel unusually nervous. I've done so many different types of audiences before. Family shows, topless bars, college frat houses, nightclub audiences, auditorium-sized crowds, stadium sized crowds, audiences of a handful of people, and crowds with bellies full of sedating food, even audiences that were all liquored up. You name it, I've done them. But this audience is sitting in wheelchairs. The bottom line is, they will smile, giggle and laugh, if it kills me. Then from the corner of my eye, I notice one particular elderly gentleman sitting at the end of the front row. Backstage earlier, I had been told that this gentleman was New Mexico's last WWI veteran. I want him to enjoy the show the most.

"Greetings one, greetings all! Boy, am I proud of the show I have for you this afternoon! But first, let's talk about who's in the news and what's in the news . . . How about that Saddam Hussein? Talk about a dude that needs sensitivity training. And I know some guys in the 82nd airborne who would be happy to give it to him." Some of the more healthy individuals in the audience roar in approval. The energy in the room begins to build.

"By the way . . . why aren't there any Walmart's in Bagdad? There are just too many Targets, that's all." The audience breaks up as more people trickle in through the front entrance. "As a matter of fact, isn't that Saddam a shady character? But we have President Bush . . ." From the stage, I can see over everyone's heads as the snow floats in through the front doors. "And, of course he's sitting in the war room with his generals, planning strategy. He's thinking that if I place these battleships equipped with Tomahawk missiles over here in the Gulf, and the B-1 Bombers over here in Saudi Arabia, I'll be able to put several hardened battalions of ground troops from ten different countries along the front lines. Equipped with gas masks, they will advance side by side with divisions of Bradly M1 tanks. Folks, Saddam will wish he worked for 7-11."

My eyes take quick notice of the WWI veteran, his American Legion cap on at a cocky tilt, sitting at the end of the front row. Still, no laugh from him. My mind snaps into another mode.

"It's tough to be President Bush right now. It really is. Especially because everybody knows where he lives and how much he makes!" Laughter builds. "As Uncle Milty, Milton Berle, says, it's tough when it comes to electing a president because we only get our pick of two candidates. But for Miss America, we get our choice of fifty!"

As the room finally breaks out solid laughter, I feel more pressure to be funny. Wheelchairs, crutches, body bandages, doctors, nurses, young men, old men, young women, mature women, people in suits and especially my own cohorts standing in the wings, all are hanging onto my every word.

"This afternoon I am proud to bring before you a variety of talent. Later, you will see your headliner, a magician, who will make me disappear. He has toured with me throughout the Southwest. Billy McCarthy is here!" I clap myself, to blatantly solicit applause. "But before you see him, I am proud to present New Mexico's own home-grown success story, the lowrider comic himself, William 'Weely' Cordova!" I milk all of the applause.

"But now, it's a great pleasure for me to introduce to you a fellow I consider to be my mentor in this business. He has brought show biz to our neck of the woods more times than I can count!" In the back of my mind I know that he is still the top convention show producer in the Southwest. During his career he brought to town Tarzan's Johnny Weissmuller, also Gypsy Rose Lee, and the original crooner, Rudy Valle, Mickey Rooney, Desi Arnaz and his big band, and Harry James and his big band. And more eclectically, the novelty acts of Tiny Tim, Twiggy, The Surf Riding Squirrel, and my personal favorite, Rocky the Boxing Kangaroo and later, his son Rambo. "He's a fellow that has seen more V.A. hospitals than any of us here today! Please put them together for the man they call Mr. Terrific, Frank Crosby!" I exit stage right, still clapping.

Frank enters from stage left palming his cheat sheet into his side jacket pocket. Calmly approaching the microphone, he stands alone, with relaxed arms down in front of him, one hand over the other. "A funny thing happened to me on the way over here this afternoon."

I listen and watch Frank from the wings. His act consists of familiar and rehashed vaudeville material. But, nevertheless, the tried and true still draws laughs.

"I said to the guy as he sat at the bar next to me, how's it going buddy?" In imitation, Frank begins to stutter, "I'm do-do- doing o-o-ok-kay, the guy said. So, I asked him, what are you drinking, buddy? He said, Be-be-beer, he finally spit out. So, I asked how long has he been stuttering? He said, All my-my li- li-life. Then I told him that I used to be a stutterer. But I got cured by making love to my wife. I told him that he should try it. Well, the next week I saw this same guy at the bar. And he still stuttered. So, I asked him if he tried my suggestion. He said that he did, but it didn't work. Then he complimented me. He told me that I had a nice house!"

The audience breaks up while Frank milks the laughs. No one notices Frank's squeaky voice now.

"A while back I was promoting hockey in this town and got in an accident. I was fooling around on the ice, and I caught a hockey puck over my right eye. I was in this hospital so they could graft some human skin over the cut. They couldn't get any human skin, so they grafted dog skin over my eye. Now when I walk past a tree, my eye winks, then it waters."

The younger pros stop their concentration in the wings to watch this seasoned veteran do his thing. Frank's enjoying the audience.

I relax in a chair stage right wing to kick back and enjoy watching my mentor.

"I've been asked if I've lived in Albuquerque all my life. I simply say, not yet! I came to Albuquerque right after World War II. It was much smaller than it is now, of course. When I was asked why I came here, I tell them I came for the asthma. And so I caught it! They ask me if I'm going to retire. I said not yet, I've been recycled."

It's fantastic to feel my audience enjoying the show, especially the WWI veteran in the front row who is finally laughing. Frank wraps up his act sooner than expected. I glance at my watch. Sure enough, he did his fifteen minutes on the dot. The grand old gentleman walks off stage right to strong applause.

I enter. "Ladies and gentlemen, that's Mr. Terrific. Keep it going for Frank Crosby." The old veteran is applauding enthusiastically. "So, now, ladies and gentlemen, from the old school to the new school. A New

Mexico comic success story. He's performed Vegas . . . New Mexico and soon the one in Nevada too! He's performed in Hollywood at the Improv and even at the rim of the   Grand Canyon! Ladies and Gentlemen, if you do not know what a lowrider is, you soon will." I change my voice to an ultra-formal delivery. "Please put them together for the most eminent lowrider comic, William Cordova, the third," exiting to the right as Weely enters from the left.

He walks up to the microphone and simply stands behind it. One, two, three beats go by before he speaks. Then, in a thick Mexican accent, "How's it going?" he asks.

I respond from the wings as prearranged, also in a thick Mexican accent, "Pretty Goot!"

The audience laughs at the play on timing.

"Oh good, there's bilingual people here. Somebody thinks we're on Johnny Carson." He wins the audience over with the first chuckle. "I've been performing for Ronn for many years. And he still screws up. My name is not William. It's Weely. Call me Weely. I'm Spanich," he says in his thick Mexican accent. "I'm a lowrider." From his rear pocket, he pulls out a plaid bandana and proceeds to tie it around his forehead. The audience laughs at his audacity.

"People accuse me of stealing batteries, jumping people." The bandana falls over his eyes. "Hey, I can't see you, how can I steal your batteries?" The audience breaks up even more, and Weely knows he's won them over.

Backstage and behind the curtain, I watch my magician headliner meticulously prepare his magic stand of tricks. Dressed in the standard magician's tuxedo, Billy McCarthy's years have taken their toll on him. In his early forties, he looks like he's in his late fifties. But one thing I know for sure, Billy is one talented magician.

I hear the audience laugh. Casually, Weely starts talking to various people sitting in the front rows. One by one he throws out a one-liner for each. Eventually he selects the vet to talk to. "How's it going, sir? And what's your name?" The smiling old gent wears his American Legion cap proudly.

"Isaha. Isaha Jones is my name," he says with a proud cowboy drawl. His large smile reveals a toothless grin.

"Sir, what kind of car do you drive? And where is it parked?" He even gets a laugh.

"I don't have a car. Haven't driven in years," came the old fellow's spunky reply. Smiles captivate the audience.

Not letting the unexpected reply catch him off guard, Weely grins. "Well, I guess I won't be stealing your battery then."

"My last car was a Chevy," Isaha says with a smile while maintaining the attention.

"Well, Isaha, what kind of Chevy did you drive?"

Snapping back with toothless pride, "A 75 Corvette Stingray, red, V-8. A thousand horses it had!"

"Hey Isaha, want to be in my gang? I'm sure my gang, Pepe won't mind. Maybe he could learn something."

***

The magician stands in front of the audience with controlled confidence as he asks the same question every magician has asked since the dawn of time, "May I have a volunteer from the audience?" Not a single hand raises. Except one. Isaha Jones waves his hand with exuberance. As if he has a choice, the magician looks around, then settles on Isaha. "Out of the throngs of thousands, I'll pick you sir. Please step up to the stage." With unexpected agility Isaha Jones walks up the side steps, unassisted. "Ladies and Gentlemen, please give him a round of applause' for coming up here." Everyone in the room watches the energized old fellow practically bounce over to stage center. "And your name, sir?"

A large group in the audience already knows his name. All humorously shout it out, "Isaha Jones!"

"All right folks. Isaha Jones, how are you sir?" He stretches out his hand to shake Isaha's with both of his. He sincerely has respect for this seasoned vet.

"Just fine and dandy," Isaha snaps back.

"Well, Isaha, please tell these fine folks what time you came up here to this stage, please."

"Why, sure enough," Isaha looks at his wrist for a watch, nothing.

"Isaha, are you looking for this?" The magician hands the watch back to him in full view of the audience.

Great relief sweeps over Isaha as the audience chuckles.

"For our first trick, ladies and gentlemen, Isaha will provide for us a one-hundred-dollar bill."

"Are you kidding, sonny? That would be a trick. I got no one hundred bucks!"

"Well how about a fifty-dollar bill Mr. Jones?" The old boy simply shakes his head. "Well, why don't you look?" Reaching into his back pocket, Isaha finds that his wallet is missing. He checks his other pocket. Another worried and concerned expression overtakes him. Billy McCarthy holds out his wallet, "Is this your wallet, Mr. Jones?" Snapping back the wallet, Isaha Jones immediately looks for his money. "So, Mr. Jones. Please pull out your money."

Isaha Jones pulls out a fifty-dollar bill.

The audience starts laughing. Isaha offers to give the fifty dollars back to McCarthy who signals Isaha just to keep it. The audience applauds strongly which cascades to the back of the room.

As Isaha moves to exit stage, Billy reaches out to him. Through the microphone he asks, "Isaha, please stay up here to help me with this." Isaha shrugs his shoulders and stays put. Billy pulls out more props while standing at stage center. Everyone watches the magician pull out a four-foot stand with a black cloth draped over it. "So Isaha, how old are you, anyway?" he banters.

"I'm ninety-two years old," Isaha says proudly. Everyone claps. "I was in the first big one, you know."

"Give Isaha another round of applause ladies and gentlemen," prompts the magician. The applause continues. "Well sir, I just happen to know that you do have a one-dollar bill in that wallet. May we borrow that?"

He nods. "That I can afford." He pulls out the bill.

"Thank you. Now put it on this table," Isaha complies. "Without showing me, write your birth date on the corner of the bill." He hands Isaha a pen. The magician writes something out of sight on a giant show card. "Now Isaha, fold that bill in two." Billy snaps his fingers and produces a lighter. He lights it. "Now Isaha, place the bill over the flame."

"You're not one of those crazy kids, are you?" laughs Isaha. Yet he does as instructed, and the crowd watches as the bill quickly goes up in flames.

From his magic stand, the illusionist pulls out a basket of lemons. "Isaha, pick one, any one."

"Whatever you say, kid," as he selects that perfect one.

Billy gives the gentleman a knife. "Now, slice it open."

As Isaha slices into the lemon, he finds an object in it. "Please show the audience what you found." All eyes in the room watch Isaha Jones carefully and meticulously unfold a dollar bill. "Now please tell the audience what is written on it," He starts toward the large reader cards that he just wrote on.

"It's my dollar. It says what I just wrote, March 3, 1899."

"Isaha, please read that bill again."

"March 3, 1899." Isaha repeats.

The magician proudly holds out the giant cards for the audience to see that he wrote March 3, 1899. The audience breaks out with a strong and approving applause. He bows, "Thank you, thank you. And how about Isaha Jones? The oldest heckler ever! Give him a round of applause." And they do.

Isaha Jones takes a bow and walks offstage and back to his chair, showing his toothless grin all the way.

After the show, many people asked old Isaha how the magician did those tricks. And, like a trooper, he never let on that he had previously consulted with Billy McCarthy and was paid that fifty-dollar bill.

Chapter Thirty

As I walk outside after the show, a gloomy shroud of gray captures the sky as the afternoon matures. It is sensed that night is coming a little earlier. I step onto crunching snow while saying my goodbyes and thanks to all of my fellow participants. Finally, sloshing to my car, I sit inside while the engine warms. Instinctively I snap on the radio. Military style, patriotic music blares out. This is eerie because I know I had the thing tuned to a rock and roll station.

My quandary is immediately answered. A weird monotone voice of the radio announcer comes on. "It is official. At 4:00 p.m. mountain standard time, CNN reports that American Air Force bombers have taken off from bases in Saudi Arabia. It is safe to assume that the war in the Persian Gulf is underway."

Chapter Thirty-One

The Shady Lady Tour

This 110 in the shade, afraid-to-touch-any-kind-of-metal-exposed-to-the-sun, kind of afternoon evaporates when I enter through spinning glass doors. I'm enveloped with lovely temperature conditioned air. I take off my sunglasses, wipe the sweat from my brow and stare at the kaleidoscope of casino activity before me.

There are flashing lights of red, green, blue and orange, along with all the bells and whistles, as far as my eyes can see. The sound of coins clanging into metal trays below slot machines, echoes. Prevalent are money carts being pushed over overly thick pile carpet by tux-shirt and tie-wearing women. A blue haired lady with a half-smoked cigarette dangling from her mouth is parked in front of not one, not two, but three push button bandits, pouring in quarters one after another. Running out of coins, she stops a money cart. After putting down her cigarette, in a gravelly voice says, "Give me fifty dollars in quarters." She continues to pour more coins into machines whose reels twirl and twirl and twirl with no matches. She curses under her breath.

I pace myself past slot machines through the Las Vegas Swan Hotel and Casino. Then by craps tables that are surrounded by dice tossing enthusiasts. I enjoy the stroll through my place of employment.

The first of tonight's four shows does not start for another couple of hours. So why rush?

"Good afternoon, Ronnie," comes a seductive lady's voice. "Good to see you back."

I spin to see a scantily clad cocktail waitress in pink silk with silver trim, only a few feet away. Her lovely smile, tanned legs, and emphasized breasts immediately catch my attention.

"Hi there. How are you?" I wish I could remember her name.

She nods and raises her tray of cocktails over her head. "Good to see you back." She maneuvers around the crowded gaming tables. One of these days, I'd like to learn her name. My eyes move to the ceiling of what seems to be acres and acres of mirrors. My gut tells me that someone up there is looking down over me. And one of these days, I'd like to take a look up there just to look down.

My attention, like many around me, is drawn to television lights suddenly snapped on at the other side of the room. Local TV news is apparently covering an event at a special side parlor poker room swarmed with people. Bright lights add heat and humidity to the attraction as it draws its crowd. An easel sign outside its doors announces Playoffs for the Million Dollar World Series of Poker.

The restaurants are next. Multiple lines of people lead into the six buffet lines. A flashing neon sign with scrawling letters over the entrances announce All You Can Eat: $2. The buffet tables offer endless cuisine selections, but I can't see an empty table. And despite the aromatic seduction, I tell myself I'll pick up something after the shows. From years of experience, I know if I eat before going on stage, I'll regret it later. Nevertheless, shrimp and chicken stay on my mind as I move closer to the showrooms.

I turn a corner. Gaming areas disappear from sight, but their exciting sounds echo down the hallway before me. Numerous showroom doorways are to my right and left. All wait to be opened tonight. Above each, marquees promote spectacular productions.

I like the marquee placement because across the front of each showroom are bold and bright lettering that tell all. The smallest showroom at the far end has the smallest marquee over the front doors. It reads: The Swan Comedy Club. A side easel sign lights up to state: Tonight! THE SHADY LADY TOUR. Under that it reads: Four Big Shows Nightly! 6:30PM, 8:00PM, 9:30PM, 11:00PM. $10.

***

The brunette, Anni Danger, a traveling pro comic based out of Hollywood, sits comfortably. Across from her, sipping a cafe mocha, is her feature act for the week, a redhead Martha Wesson. Taking a bite from a flour tortilla with red chile off a plate of Huevos Rancheros is their MC, the Chicana humorist, blonde (this week), Silver Vega. The hustle and bustle of the busy casino restaurant encompasses them.

"So Anni, how long have you been doing comedy?" asks Martha.

Anni sips her cup of coffee, "It has to be at least ten years now," she says. "But I got to admit, it was a lot easier for a lady comic to start back then, than it is now. I seem to remember more opportunity."

Both Silver Vega and Martha Wesson hang on their present mentor's every word. This is a unique chance to learn from a successful lady professional.

"Doesn't traveling every week to earn a paycheck—especially out of Hollywood—get to you?" asks Silver.

"Absolutely not! Men have been doing it for years! I love the fact that someone else makes up my hotel bed every morning. Somebody else even cooks my meals! Plus, I can still be in L.A. when opportunity calls. Especially if you want some TV action." Martha and Silver listen to her intently. "You have to be there for the audition seasons. That's where you have to be if you want to be seen by all the TV people, especially the Carson people. I'm sure the new Leno people will be the same. There's a new life's blood happening there."

Martha has to ask, "Isn't it easier to get started from the other side of the country, though." Silver nods at the same time.

Anni Danger replies, "Well that's because out there, a comic doesn't have to travel so far between gigs like out here in the southwest. You still have to play clubs every week. But back there, they're only a few hours apart, normally." She takes another sip.

As the coffee cups cool down, Martha waves over a handsome waiter. "Some more, please," she raises her cup to him. "Doesn't this make you a hard person?" she asks Danger while she eyes the waiter's crotch with a devilish smile.

"Well, anyone in this business that knows Anni Danger knows I love everyone. But I will not put up with any bullshit. This is a backstabbing business as it is, and I don't like adding to it." She anticipates her cup of java as the waiter pours into it.

As the waiter walks away, all three ladies' eyes zoom in on his backside. They acknowledge their view with mutual smiles.

"Is this week an unusual week, being an all lady comic lineup?" wonders Silver. I know you've played all over the country in all the AAA clubs and all. Have you seen this before? Because when I was living back east, I seldom saw a night filled with all ladies. I was told it was kind of taboo at the box office."

"That can be true. But occasionally I do see some all lady lineups out in Southern California way. So, you got to give Ronn a little credit for having the balls to try it. I hear he gives his ladytalents more than their share of breaks."

Silver shoots in, "But I remember years ago when Ronn and I started in this biz together, he hated putting me on stage. He was still in that male macho frame of mind back then. But he's come around. It's still why he's billing us this week as the Shady Lady Tour. It's that macho instinct of his."

"Well, I told him that the next time he brings us together, I want him to bill our shows, The Butt Load of Babes Tour," says the Hollywood headliner. They laugh.

"Yeah, but all I know is that if it wasn't for Ronn, I wouldn't have developed as fast as I have," Martha says.

Silver says, "I was in Ronn's very first comedy show many years ago. I've occasionally left the biz while I pursued my jewelry manufacturing on the side. And then with my travels from New York to L.A., I eventually came back to Albuquerque, and there he is, still at it."

***

The band on the side stage of the Vegas comedy club showroom rehearse top 40 rock and roll tunes from the 70s and 80s. I quietly slip inside through the darkened entrance a couple of hours before show time. Wanting to go unnoticed, I sit in the shadows of the top row of tables.

My showman instincts dictate that the band Untouchables open for my show of stand-up comics. Typically it is the other way around. The band polishes their routine. I've heard them countless times before. But maybe it's because I just enjoy watching Nancy, their lead singer. She'd be a twelve in a bikini contest if it was filled with tens. I haven't had the opportunity to tell her I've returned.

As the producer of this show, months ago I felt it was a little expensive but a brilliant idea to add live music support to the comedy show. With every casino in this town having their own comedy club, I wanted to give the patrons a little more for their entertainment buck. The moment an audience enters the showroom, the band strikes it up. High energy rock-n-roll of sing-along hits straight off the charts whips up the crowd to a fever pitch. This builds the crescendo that opens the show.

Then, as the comics enter and exit the stage, musical riffs escort them on and off. After the show, the band kicks up again as the crowds exit.

It's been a successful experiment and I'm looking forward to telling Jose, Javier, Jim and especially lovely Nancy that I'll be extending their contracts.

As the band rehearses, I recline in a lounge chair in the rear shadows of the darkened, air-conditioned showroom. My mind wanders. On my first night back in more than a month, I cannot help but recapture the event that led to this moment.

Chapter Thirty-Two

It's been a year today since my Chrysler La Baron drove west on Route 66 out of Flagstaff. I love, love Flag. But after a couple of years in that Arizona college town, the Monte Vista comedy room finally closed due to a combination of factors. Back and forth weekly travel between Albuquerque contributed. Plus, memories of Georgette haunted me. So, I took on a local assistant to help run things so I wouldn't have to come to Flagstaff every week. And that backfired.

An ad sales rep for the local TV station was a sharp enough cookie to take on the demands. After months of showing her the ropes, she developed her own ideas. Unbeknownst to me, she began to think it would be easier to produce her own comedy show at another nightclub in town that was buying more ad time from her, and she became a competitor without giving me any notice. My client, the Monte Vista, got nervous on me. Suddenly, they were dealing with an unexpected competitor that I had inadvertently given birth to.

My competitor opened with open-mic caliber comics, while the Route 66 talent were all professionals. Nevertheless, the sudden glut of live comedy in the little town proved to be oversaturation, which killed the market for both clubs as both closed. So, life moves on. And so did I.

The Route 66 turning point came in Kingman, Arizona. Stopped at the main red light in the middle of town, I looked right toward Las Vegas, and then left toward Death Valley, California. I tapped my finger on the steering wheel, oblivious to the car horns blasting behind me.

As far as I was concerned, I had nothing waiting for me at either destination. I'd have to start from scratch no matter where I went. Only then did I see the billboard right in front of my face, hiding in plain sight:

LAS VEGAS, NEVADA, THE ENTERTAINMENT CAPITOL OF
THE WORLD!

It was a no brainer as I turned north. Confidence in my decision only
came at my first glimpse of the majestic Hoover Dam and the grand
body of water it held back, Lake Mead. As I drove across the damn, I
made a goal of conquering that 24-hour town.

Upon my arrival, life—to my amazement—was an instant success.
The first thing I did was check the want ads in the local paper. There in
bold black and white: Wanted Comedy Club Assistant Manager. With
my pro comedy club production background, I was hired on the spot.
Within a couple of months, the club manager resigned to take a similar
job in Atlantic City.

Success with the show was immediate. It was only a few months later that I realized what I had inherited from my predecessor. The show's
real success was based on the established booking and marketing plans
already in place. By the time this realization hit, I have already succumbed to the Vegas wildlife.

I was always the front man and proud and cocky enough to make
sure everyone knew it. This was a natural lead to receiving invites to
every party in town. Bikini clad pool parties and 5:00 a.m. penthouse
soirees accompanied multiple days of debauchery at every mansion in
town. And then came the first six month raise.

It was the largest paycheck I had ever made. I immediately squan-
dered it. I leased a penthouse apartment. Next, I leased a Cadillac
convertible. Soon came the usual sex, drugs and rock-n-roll requirements
of my playboy existence. Then came the crash.

Summer turned into autumn when a long, warm October night
changed into dawn by the time I hit the sack about 6:00 a.m. The phone
cut through my afternoon slumber.

"Answer the thing, why don't you," came a female voice next to me. Through my liquor-soaked brain I seem to remember her telling me that she was a dancer with the Follies Bergère show. Her name's Dana, I think. We met last night at a party in some unknown penthouse. These are the only facts that snap into place.

The phone rings again before I reach over her bare breasts to the bed stand next to her. The digital clock reads 3:05 p.m. The sun was shining through the crack between the closed curtains.

"Hello, Ronn. It's Bob."

It's my brother, Robert. I haven't talked with him since I left Albuquerque on a visit one month ago. "Hey, man, what's happening?" I yawn while I wake up.

"Dad had a stroke this morning. He's in the V.A."

I jump into a sitting position. "How did it happen? I mean, how is he?"

"It's serious man. Can you break away? He's unable to talk or communicate, but you know he'd want you here."

"Yeah, right! I'll call you right back with flight arrangements." My gut starts to churn. It's the first time since Mom died that I have felt this.

Ignoring the undraped, sleek, muscle-toned redheaded fem fatal stretched out next to me, I start making phone calls. By the time I speak with the Manager on Duty at the hotel to explain everything, Dana has started to dress. By the time I call the showroom's stage manager to ask him to cover for me, she is brushing her hair and putting on makeup. By the time I phone the airline, she kisses me on the cheek.

"Thank you for understanding, darling," I tell her. And, as I make my reservation on the next flight to Albuquerque, she's opening the front door.

As the penthouse door snapped shut behind her, she probably knew we'd never see each other again.

Chapter Thirty-Three

A huge orange and red fireball hovers over the western plateau. It prepares to sink behind Albuquerque's distant dormant volcanos on the western horizon. No one answers when I call home. So, I call a cab to pick me up from the Albuquerque International Sunport and take me directly to the Veteran's Hospital. What a coincidence. I'm now visiting my father in the same hospital where I did those comedy benefits last winter.

I carry one shoulder-harnessed bag as I track down my father's room on the fifth floor. Going up in the elevator, I think about dad being in the VA Hospital, of all places.

Relieved to have finally found the right ward, I pass through a long sterile hallway to the nurse's station. Behind her on the wall is a full patient roster. Sure enough, there it read GRECO, JULIAN, bed A2.

"Hello. My name is Ronn Greco. I've come to see my father, Julian Greco."

"Visiting hours are over for the day. Come back tomorrow."

"But I just flew in from out-of-town as soon as I heard about my dad. How is he?"

"Feel assured that Mr. Greco is resting comfortably. The doctor will be here in the morning if you care to speak with him then."

Frustration builds. I linger. My heart beats faster. The hustle and bustle of the last five hours is catching up with me, and I'm pissed. But knowing how my voice would bounce off these slick walls, I take a deep breath and keep silent. But barely.

"Please, nurse." I glance at her name tag, "Jean? Jean I was only notified five hours ago that my father had a stroke. Flying in from Vegas to get here only minutes after visiting hours are over is cruel, don't you think?" I wait for her response but get none. "Please don't dismiss me. Please let me see my father!"

The second nurse with an aura of authority comes out from a back office, "You are Mr. Greco's son?" I nod. "If I remember right, didn't you promote some benefit comedy shows here last winter?"

"Yes, that's right," I don't want to talk shop. "Can you at least tell me how my father's really doing?"

She takes Nurse Jean aside. Jean quickly returns to the desk with an obvious change of attitude. "Mr. Greco, we will make an exception in your case. You will still have to speak with the doctor in the morning. But I will show you to your father's bedside."

Farther down the hallway and then to my right, I keep step with Nurse Jean. Her steps are soft and silent. Mine are hard and anxious as they echo off the freshly painted walls. I'm relieved that Dad is in this modern, newly built hospital. But the antiseptic-alcohol hospital smell is familiar. All hospitals must smell the same.

"Your father has had many concerned visitors in the last hours," the nurse says. "He must have many friends and a big family."

Finally we arrive at the last room at the end of the corridor. Two of its four beds are empty. The other patient watches the TV with the audio lightly coming out of the remote control box across his bed. In the far corner, only a small light hangs over Dad's bed.

With great trepidation, I approach my father. A spider's web of tubes lead from both of his wrists, veins, mouth and nose. Various monitors surround the bed. All have their own cables attached to my father's body. Other than that, he seems to be stretched out comfortably.

"If you need me, push this button." The nurse wraps the cable of the TV/radio/security remote control box around the bed's side security bars. Then she leaves us.

Dad's silver hair is neatly combed, and it is obvious that he is resting peacefully. As memory serves me, when I was sick, Dad stood over me concerned like this.

"Dad, it's me, Ronn. I've come home. Can you hear me?" There is no visual response. Tears well up in my eyes as I place my palm over my father's forehead. "Ah, Pop . . . Dad, I love you. I want you to know that I love you." I brush back my father's silver hair.

The silence of the hospital floor is somehow deafening.

***

Days go by. Then a week becomes two weeks. I begin to realize that this situation will not be coming to a quick solution.

Pop lies comfortably asleep and propped up in his bed. His right side is limp and useless. Each time he wakes, he tries to mouth some words, but only guttural sounds emit. It hurts to see the frustration in his face. I pour him a cup of water. When dinner is served about five o'clock, I pull in all my patience to slowly spoon the food into his mouth. Great care is necessary to wipe his mouth with the napkin.

Around six o'clock comes the changing of the guard. Bob arrives from his daily work at the University of New Mexico library. This is the rare moment each day when Julian Greco has his two sons together. Both of us are happy to see our father manage a difficult smile.

We develop a daily routine. I stay with him from midafternoon till my brother arrives. Robert stays till visitor's hours expire each evening. Both of us take comfort in knowing that our uncles, early risers that they are, arrive when the doors open in the morning. They help with breakfast, then lunch. Along the way, many relatives and dad's friends visit. This activity has contributed to dad's slow but steady recovery, a little each day.

As for me, everyday difficulties and job pressure start to build. However, I need to stay in Albuquerque despite the fact that my job requires my presence in another state.

I maintain a semblance of managing my Las Vegas showroom using long distance day and night phone calls, but it gets more complicated as each day passes. When the cat is away, the comic mice do play.

Leaving the showroom house manager in charge in my absence was a good idea, initially. But as time goes by and, as the house manager did his own job as well as mine, problems arise.

Scheduling talents and fee negotiations are part of my job. One conversation usually can settle any concerns, but when I'm not available, inaccurate information gets conveyed, and trouble happens. When media promotions are scheduled and I'm not there to carry them out, things can get difficult. A comic or two have been showing up late or a week early. Problems are mounting, not to mention the low morale. And, although I'm two states away, I'm still responsible. At this rate, how long will I still be responsible? This is trouble, trouble, trouble. I have to be in Vegas to handle my business, not in Albuquerque of all places. But gazing at my father's helpless body, I know where I must be.

Yesterday, I had to sign a medical release. It stated that if dad's situation no longer benefited by any future medical care, permission is given to simply make dad comfortable. I knew what that meant but didn't want to admit it.

For now, Bob arrives for the changing of the guard. It's time to go home to make my second round of daily Vegas updates. While Dad sleeps comfortably, I leave the V.A. Hospital room I've grown to know all too well.

No sooner do I step inside the old homestead than the phone greets me. I sense who is calling. "Hello, Ronn Greco here."

"Ronn, we got a problem here," comes a frantic voice.

"Hello, Aaron. How are you?" I insist on the gracious formality.

"Yeah, hi. We got a problem. The headliner this week, Guy Thomas, says there's a discrepancy in his money."

"Guy Thomas?"

"He says his contract was for more money than we paid him. He's making a stink about it."

"Was he partying heavy this week?"

"Are you kidding? He's been Mr. Hookers and Booze all week."

"When he was pushing me for the booking, I told him that he wasn't going to stiff me with his party bill like he did last time. He has a habit of doing that."

"Well, he's a party animal that's for sure."

"Okay. Tell him that arrangements have been made to have his liquor and food costs automatically deducted from his check. Don't let him bluff you, either. He has a silver tongue when it comes to that. How did he do on stage?"

"He killed 'em. He got a standing ovation a couple of nights ago. If there's a problem, I'll call you."

"If he gives you any crap, tell him to call me. To avoid his schmooze, which he will try, tell him that if he wants to be treated like Dangerfield, he should draw crowds like Dangerfield. We'll undoubtedly talk later." We both hang up. No sooner do I make my way to my makeshift office at the back of the house when the phone rings again. "Hello, Greco here."

"Mr. Greco? Brent Steivesen here."

The casino's General Manager has been calling once a week as a routine. But this is the third time he's called this week. "Yes sir. Greetings to you, sir."

He shows a bit of his Bostonian upper crust accent by asking, "How is your father's recovery? Showing improvement, we hope?"

"Dad's hanging in there. He's a fighter, that's for sure. We're hoping he'll be ready for therapy soon."

"Well, we're hoping that he is doing so well that you will be able to return to the SWAN soon. You've been gone what, three or four weeks now?"

"That's right sir. Almost a month."

"That's right. It has been pushing a month, has it not? And it has come to my attention that you have occasionally been hard to contact. A growing number of situations pertaining to the comedy club are being brought to my attention. More often than I care for. Normally I understand that you keep these concerns pretty much in control. But lately, I feel it's grown more necessary for me to oversee their resolution in your absence. Quite frankly, this is not why this casino has a comedy club director. I should not have to be confronted with the club's day-to-day operation. I understand that last night your headliner had to be bailed out of incarceration."

"What? I didn't know that! Guy Thomas was in jail?"

"If it wasn't for the MOD receiving his call from downtown this morning to provide funds to secure his release, he would not be available to go on stage tonight. That is a fact."

"Who was the manager on duty?" I had to ask.

"He just started a week ago and comes to us from Atlantic City. He handled the situation well. But the point is, he should not have had to handle it at all."

"Yes, sir. The doctors say that my father's progressing and they have him closely monitored. And if things continue like this, I hope to be back at the casino in a week." I hate being pressured to commit myself.

"Fine. We do wish you the best in this difficult time. But to be straightforward, I cannot continue to cover the situation. Your employment requires you to be on the job."

"Thank you, sir." I close my eyes. My skull throbs.

"We hope to see you soon back on the job, good luck."

"I appreciate it sir, good-bye." My white knuckle grip on the phone receiver strains. I feel like slamming the phone down. Only then do I notice the flashing light on my answering machine indicating twenty-two messages. I reluctantly press the playback button. Slumping into the chair behind my desk, I massage my temples. Fingertips rub, rub deep worry lines in my forehead.

Chapter Thirty-Four

After all is said and done, I count fourteen messages from national comics wanting bookings or changes in schedules. Six calls are from my stage manager. But one message is so sweet, it's the only call I am happy to receive.

"Hello, Ronnie. This is Nancy. I am so, so sorry to miss you again this week. I am really sorry to hear about your father. I wish I could be there to help you with what you must be going through. But our band is doing fine. I want you to know that your Vegas house band is one thing you don't have to worry about. I'll call you again next week. Take care, sweetie."

My stress turns to a smile as the machine snaps off. If I could have romance in mind at this time, she would be the recipient of all of my attention. That girl has proven to be special. But it's the next message that most concerns me, from Dad's doctor.

He speaks in a monotone, matter of fact voice. "Mr. Greco? I want to confirm your signature of power of attorney on a series of hospital admission documents. And in particular, the release you signed yesterday for the go-ahead to cease treatment and simply make the patient comfortable in the last hours in the event that nothing more can be done."

I look at my watch. It's 8:00 p.m., sharp. In the past, the doc has been accessible between 6:00 a.m. to 3:00 p.m. So, I'll call him in the morning for clarification. Right now, I'm drained. Normally, if I was in Vegas, I'd be up and going and just starting at this hour, but the day's events have taken a toll on my bones. After an hour or so spent returning long distance phone calls, I hear my brother come home through the side door. That means it's time to take a shower and hit the sack. My heavy head hits the pillow already asleep. The bedside clock reads 9:30 p.m. My second show of the evening in Vegas should be well underway by now.

In my sleep, a distant phone rings. The ringing persists, wearing down my slumber. I toss and turn under the sheets, briefly opening my eyes as the ringing finally stops. So, I figure that the answering machine caught it. But it starts up again, and louder. It forces me to fully open my eyes. The bedside clock reads 1:30 a.m.

My brother's television still blares. Brother Bob learned a while ago that phone calls at this early hour are usually Comedy Club, and he lets the answering machine get them.

After being scolded by the casino GM for not being accessible, I'd better answer it. Probably some comic problem again. The shows should have been over at this hour, anyway.

By the time my feet touch the carpet, the answering machine takes another message. I stumble across the house to play back the messages. The phone rings again. Through grogginess, my hand lifts the receiver on the half ring. "Hello."

"Yes, I'm trying to reach a Ronn Greco," comes a serious voice.

Yawning. "Yeah, that's me."

"I am Doctor Heathcliff from the Veteran's Hospital. Are you the son of Julian Greco?"

"Yes, sir. Yes."

"Mr. Greco, I regret to inform you that your father passed at twelve hours, six minutes this morning. You may be interested in knowing he was comfortable and in his sleep."

"Uh, uh . . ." the impact yet to hit. "My father died? He was doing fine when I left him around five o'clock tonight?"

"Sir, his system, being on in years, simply wore down."

I am numb.

"We advise that you contact who you must. We also note here that your father has a couple of brothers to contact in case of emergency. If you'd like, I can call them now."

The lump in my throat seems to be growing fast. "That will not be necessary, doctor. I'll take it from here."

"My condolences to your family."

Before I realize it, I'm in my brother's smoke-filled bedroom. The TV news is on when I tell my brother about the one man we both loved.

Chapter Thirty-Five

Countless rows of white tombstones in meticulous perpetual care recede in geometrical tiers up slopes of green manicured lawns of the Veteran's National Cemetery in Santa Fe, New Mexico. A parked funeral procession lines the winding path that surrounds the final resting place of an old soldier, my Pop.

Six American Legion pall bearers rest an American flag-draped casket over an altar in the graveyard chapel. Soon, Dad's casket will join the resting place with his waiting wife. A Catholic priest waits to pray those last words. My brother, Bob, and cousin, Diane, sit by my side. Countless friends, relatives and best wishers place flowers on the casket.

My strained, red, cried-out eyes watch the priest's lips move in a sermon, but I hear nothing. I just remember my Dad, who soon will be resting with Mom, once again. Eighty-one-years old, the tough old guy was. As a veteran of the Bataan Death March in World War II, he survived a sixty-five-mile forced march and endured the entire war in a Japanese prisoner of war camp.

Coming home, he married a bride fifteen years younger and proceeded to raise a loving, well rounded family of rambunctious boys. That was not easy. I remember being more than a handful. Yet, he taught his sons the same fortitude it took to survive WWII as a POW for almost five years. Now, I feel confident that Pop left me with the genes it takes to live a long, long life.

The loud volley of three rifles, firing twice into the air, their six gun salute, snaps me back to reality. Immediately, over a loudspeaker, a trumpet blows taps. This gut-wrenching, beautiful piece of sad music causes all three of us sitting relatives to bow our heads, unable to hold back our tears. Julian Greco's American Legion color guard removes the flag from the casket. With military precision, they sharply wrap it into the triangle fold, then present it to the veteran's son, me.

Chapter Thirty-Six

Within forty-eight hours, I'm back at the demands of the multi-colored flashing neon lights of the Vegas casino that is my employer—the last place I'm in the mood to be. But the way I figure, it could be a way to get grief off my mind. Besides, the pressures of getting back to work are compelling and simple: I don't want to get fired.

So, I'm back, and it feels like nothing has changed. The club still has its schedule to fulfill, showrooms to attract the customers only to usher them back out to the gaming areas. Get them in, get them out! Get them in, get them out!

Tonight's shows are sold out. This is always the best news to hear in show biz. Even with all the positive vibrations and excitement, this is still the last place I want to be. I still hurt. Sometimes I think I can hear Dad's voice calling me. I feel guilty being around all of this jovial activity, but I have no choice.

To add insult to injury, I can't unburden myself to anyone. Because it's my job to get the people around me pumped up for the show, not to bring them down with my grief. No one is to know otherwise.

Standing backstage, I glance at my watch. It's officially showtime! From the backstage telephone, I give the cue to the tech booth to start. Immediately the house goes dark. The follow-spotlight twirls around the room, finally landing on Nancy, lead singer of the Untouchables. This is the band's cue to start their fifteen minute pre-show presentation. Top 40 tunes energize the showroom as people enter.

On cue, the lady comics report backstage to what I call "on deck." My headliner from Hollywood, Anni Danger, is always the first to arrive, even though she is the last to go on. That's the pro in her. But I read an unusual concern on her face as she walks up and kisses my cheek.

"I'm so happy to see you back, darling. My sympathies for your loss."

I read the sincerity in her eyes.

"Thank you, sweetheart. But no need for depressing thoughts, we have a full house out there. What do you think about that?"

Martha Wesson enters through the backstage door with an overly concerned expression. She walks up and takes my hand. "I hate to give you bad news when this is the first time I've seen you in such a long time, Ronnie. But we've got a problem . . ."

The music volume lowers. The band's drummer, Jim, makes the first of his announcements that build up to the beginning of the comedy show. "Welcome, ladies and gentlemen to the SWAN Comedy Club. Our comedy show begins in only a few minutes. Now is the time to order your favorite cocktail beverages. Count 'em down, only ten minutes to a night filled with smiles, giggles and laughs. In the meantime, we are the Untouchables!"

"Silver just fell down some steps coming here," Martha says. "I think she turned her ankle."

"How is she?"

"Two hotel bellmen assisted her to her room. She couldn't walk without pain. You'd better call her."

Again, looking at my watch, I pick up the backstage phone and ask to be patched through to Silver Vega's room. It rings several times.

"Hello! Hello! Silver?"

"Oh, Ronn. I hurt myself bad!" she cries. "My ankle hurts really bad," she says through tears. "I can't put any weight on it . . . I don't think I can MC the show tonight. I can't walk."

"I'm really, really sorry to hear this especially right now, darling! We've got a full house tonight!" I'm already trying to solve this dilemma.

Again, the band lowers their volume underneath Nancy's announcement. "Five minutes, five minutes to a night filled with smiles, giggles and laughs!" The blonde highlights in her brown hair shine under the spotlight. Again, the Untouchables pick up the tempo, volume and energy.

I clutch the phone receiver, "Silver, are you sure you won't be able to MC?"

"I'm sorry, but I can't even walk. Don't be mad at me, please. I'll make it up to you," she cries in pain.

"Don't worry about that. Don't worry. Just raise your ankle. Get room service to bring up a bunch of ice, stick your foot into it. Hopefully you can MC tomorrow night. We'll come see you after the show."

Who's going to replace the MC? I've got four hundred people in the showroom. That's eight hundred eyes watching the stage. The band is building to its intro climax only minutes away. And now the Shady Lady Tour has no blonde Mistress of Ceremonies.

"Can Silver come out and play?" asks the nervous headliner, Anni Danger.

I shake my head while I think. But all I can think of is that I just got back. What if I wasn't here?

"What are we going to do?" asks Martha.

I want to leave. I sincerely wish I was not here right now. But I am here, so I pick up the phone to the tech booth. "Deliver this quick message to Jim the drummer. We have a lineup change." My two female comics are relieved when they hear me relay the solution.

"I guess my idea of naming the show the Butt Load of Babes Tour was a good idea while it lasted," says Anni Danger.

"But, you gotta do, what you gotta do," agrees Martha.

"I need a few moments to myself, ladies." They immediately leave. Building adrenaline forces me to ignore my gut-wrenching grief. "Damn! This is the last place on God's Earth I want to be right now." I switch to thinking all things funny. There's an audience out there that cannot suspect or catch a glint of my depression. The knot in my stomach grows tighter. Now, I have to make the world laugh! This, after having arranged dad's funeral only days ago.

As the seconds tick closer to showtime, the two lady comics proceed with their own personal pre-show rituals. Martha studies palm-sized paper notes, silently mouthing her act. Anni Danger impatiently paces the floor toward the back wall, out of the way.

With their volume up and the energy high, the Untouchable's drummer, Jim, delivers his last introduction. Reading from a handwritten three-by-five card just handed to him, he says, "And now Ladies and Gentlemen . . . The SWAN Comedy Club in Las Vegas, Nevada is proud to present the Shady Lady Tour plus One!"

Standing in the darkened stage wing, only mere feet from audience view, I bow my head and make my Catholic sign of the cross. I whisper to myself, "Dad, I love you and I dedicate this show to you."

The band builds musical energy to the ultimate crescendo, "So, please, with a healthy round of applause, welcome your MC and our show's producer, Ronn Greco!"

With all my inner fortitude and theatrical training, I take a deep, quick breath. Instantly my smiling persona snaps into place as I walk onto the stage and into the waiting spotlight.

The audience applauds as I skip across stage with a cheerful enthusiasm. I feel their eyes on me as I pass by the microphone that's situated stage center and continue across the stage toward the bandstand. Reaching for Nancy's hand with gallantry, I kiss it. As I bow to the band in grand recognition, they continue to play till their cue—which is when the MC, whoever it is, stops to grab the microphone.

"The Untouchables, ladies and gentlemen. Aren't they great? And how about Nancy? Isn't she lovely? I'm in love with her, don't you know." I blow her a kiss. "Give the Untouchables another round of applause, ladies and gentlemen!" I let the applause build up, then lower away.

"Folks, are you ready for a night filled with smiles, giggles and laughs?" I grin from ear to ear with my arms stretched out wide. "Well, give yourselves a round of applause for being at the right place at the right time tonight!"

Ronn takes a moment to examine the faces in his audience. One, two, three beats go by before he says anything. "Already, I see smiling faces from every boy and girl in this audience. You make me feel great . . ."

Chapter Thirty-Seven

Two years later

A sunny, crisp Indian summer afternoon offers blue skies with white puffs hovering over Interstate Forty/ Route Sixty-Six through Albuquerque, New Mexico. Bumper to bumper, five lanes of traffic shoot fifty-five plus miles an hour easterly toward the majestic mountain range that borders the city.

Halfway through town, an off ramp diverts a flow of cars, vans, trucks and motorcycles south. As they come upon a green light, most continue to drive on through while a few turn left on the first boulevard and away from speed. A slow right on the first street and one will drive into a peaceful neighborhood with kids throwing a football and bicyclists rolling down the sidewalks. The mature street is lined with tall elm trees, grassy lawns, sidewalks edged with hedges that seem to lead to one particular red brick driveway at the end of the block. Its three parking spaces hold vehicles with license plates originating in California, New York and New Mexico.

This older but freshly remodeled home has beige stucco and a shingled roof with an archway over the walkway between the house and garage. Under the archway, a new gate swings open to a brick footpath that leads to a grove of three or four elm trees filled with golden leaves ready to fall with a slight breeze. Some already cover the welcoming courtyard. A patio table with an open umbrella shields sun glare for the man sitting under it. Deep in thought, he studies a road atlas. With a swig from his bottled water, he calculates mileage between two points on the map, as he waits for the appointment with his producer. It's not difficult for him to almost make out key words of conversation emitting through a screen door only a few steps away. Above the entrance, a sign states OFFICE. The screen door is the only filter for the aroma of an Antonio & Cleopatra cigar and a conversation between two voices that waft through it. The man enjoys the warmth and sunlight as another autumn leaf falls in front of him.

One of the two voices inside comes from the black female comic, Robin Cee. She sits on the sofa saying, "It was great working with you again, Ronn."

At the opposite end of the room, I face her from behind my desk. On the wall behind me, hanging like the hundred pound light fixture that it is, a neon turquoise sign exclaims:

ROUTE SIXTY-SIX COMEDY

"You know it's always a pleasure to bring you through. You are like a sister to me," I am happy to tell her.

Robin laughs. "This tour was especially eventful. That Roswell gig was well timed. I don't know if that UFO really crashed outside that town, but I do know that there aren't too many six-foot-one black women walking around there. They were all staring at me as if I was the alien!"

I can't help but laugh myself with her at the thought. "And then, driving up to your gig in Santa Fe," she says, "I took the opportunity to go a little farther up north to the warm springs of that Sanctuary at Chimayo."

I listen intently to my headliner.

"You know I have problems with my knees. Well, not long after I waded in those pools of water up to here," she brings her hand up to mid chest, "my bony knees immediately felt better. They haven't hurt since. Then doing the gig at the Hotel Loretto, I had to visit next door to that

179

connected church just to see that spiral staircase. You know the one? Apparently, it was built more than a hundred and twenty years ago without any nails!"

I nod, smiling.

"I went in after closing last night and told the caretaker who I was, so he let me climb to the top. It was so inspirational. It seemed that I was feeling the power of the Lord through me. It was fantastic!"

"I have always thought of you as a spiritual person."

She smiles. "I can't tell you how great it left me feeling. And I'm Baptist!" I laugh again. "Did you know that the Santa Fe room is the only club in the country right next door to a church?" I stand up to walk around the desk. "Anyway, I got to get going. Thanks for the opportunity to swing through your circuit, Ronn."

I reach for her hand. "I can't tell you darling how much I appreciate you working my Billy the Kid Circuit. All the old gang of grizzled veterans I started out with are now burning out left and right! It's a pleasure to work with the young bloods like you who have the fire in their belly to hit the road."

Robin laughs. "It's gas. But I know what you mean. The road does it to you."

"Remember Mickey Finn, your fellow San Franciscan?"

"Yeah of course! His wife gave him the ultimatum. Her and the six kids or comedy!"

"Hey, it was his Irish Catholic thang, you know what I mean?" We hug, my face is eye level with her ample bosom. "Thank you for per-forming for my circuit, darling. I'll call you next month for those gigs at the ski resort."

"You should get online with some internet service. I can send you email updates on my new laptop from any phone plug from wherever I am." She opens the screen door.

"Yes ma'am. It's about time I utilize modern technology, anyway. From all I hear, it's the next wave of advancement."

As she leaves, she waves through the screen door, "And Happy Thanksgiving! I'll make sure to say hello to our mutual amigos back home. Take care."

I stretch and yawn. Sitting twelve hours a day, most of them on the phone, is getting to me. I need a life. The chiming from the Brick phone spins me around. My eyes fall on the filing cabinets behind my desk, filled with comedian files. I've got to clean them up, update them. The Brick rings again. I can fill any gig within fifteen minutes from that cabinet. But I want to cut it down to ten minutes.

I press the button on the cell. "Hello. Ronn Greco here."

Outside, Robin smiles at the stranger under the patio table umbrella.

"Are you Robin Cee out of Oakland?" he asks.

"Yes, I am. But I'm working my way to Florida. Just got back from Ronn's Roswell UFO gig last night . . ."

He offers his hand, "I'm Bart Levy, comic out of Brooklyn."

"Happy Thanksgiving, Bart Levy, comic out of Brooklyn. Nice to meet ya," she answers as a golden leaf floats onto her brown hair.

"I'm on my annual cross country Southern California trip," he says, "so, I thought I'd stop off to see the godfather, pay my respects, you know?"

"I bet you really came here just because you need to make a pit stop didn't ya?" Robin teases. "All the comics do when they pass through town. This place is handy."

He nods. "You don't know me, but I know you. Whenever I work for Ronn, I seem to follow you the next week into his rooms. Apparently, I'm doing it again. You're a hard act to follow, ya know that?"

"Thanks for the compliment." Another golden leaf glides past her. "It seems that we're two ships passing in this autumn afternoon. Are you following me into Ronn's Billy the Kid Circuit around Clovis Air Force Base?"

Bart Levy nods as both comics hear the phone ring inside. "Sounds like the godfather is busy," he says.

"I've been doing shows for Ronn for years, and that guy always seems to be slugging away at it."

Bart nods. "Well, if he didn't, guys like me wouldn't be working, that's for sure."

"Yeah, but he needs more free time. He works too hard."

Levy nods again in acknowledgment. He gets up, "Well Robin, I sincerely hope that we will be able to work together sometime soon."

Both shake hands. She walks on down the brick path between the house and garage. He proceeds to knock on the screen door.

Chapter Thirty-Eight

With my cell phone in one hand and a cordless landline phone over my other ear, I wave him in. I gesture for him to sit on the sofa across from my desk.

"That's right," I say into the phone. "Three nights in West Texas leads into a two night stand down south in El Paso, which then leads into four nights north to Santa Fe, New Mexico . . . Yeah, you can link up with your gigs in Denver. . . . Then it's an easy swing back home for you to Chicago . . . mmm . . . That's right. So, get back with me by this time tomorrow . . ." Another call on the Brick phone rings. "Please hold, Chicago." I press the hold button to answer the other phone.

"Greetings . . . Yes, this is the Route Sixty-Six Comedy Club."

Bart Levy continues to watch.

"That's right. I hire comics. You're a comic? Where are you calling from, Seattle? Hold on sir, I got Chicago on the other line. "Bart patiently waits by studying all the pictures and posters plastered over the walls and ceiling. "On second thought Seattle, I'd appreciate it greatly if you could please give me a call back in thirty minutes." As I juggle the phones, "Let me get off." I smile at Bart Levy and place my hand over the receiver, "Great to see ya Bart. Hold on." I close up with Chicago to speak into the other hand. "Yes. I'm back. Sorry to keep you waiting, sir. What's your name again? Okay, Jake out of Chicago, how many minutes do you do strong?" The visiting New Yorker's ear's perk up. "Yeah. Are you an opener, feature or a headliner?" The Brick rings again. "Excuse me for a moment while I answer this other call."

I switch over. "Hello . . . Hi, sweetheart . . . I'm happy to hear you're back." Bart smiles at my softened voice. "Where are you performing tonight? Mmmm . . . I missed you and want you back in my arms where you belong . . . Hold on. I'm on the other line with Chicago." I press the hold button on the Brick, then depress the hold button on the cordless.

"I'm back. Sorry to keep you waiting, sir. What's your name again, sir? Okay, Jake, how many minutes do you do? Strong fifteen minutes? Then you're an opener or an MC?" I have a lovely lady waiting on the other phone. "Well, I'm booked for the next ninety days, so send me your promo pack with the usual photos, resume and video," I say. "Yeah, that's right, send it to the Albuquerque, New Mexico address. Mmm . . . mm . . . You can't spell Albuquerque? How do you expect me to book you if you can't even spell the town you're calling? Oh, okay." I begrudgingly spell Albuquerque.

Bart Levy smirks and smiles at me. I can tell he remembers a couple of years ago and our first phone conversation. He was calling me from New York, and he too had to ask for the spelling. It's my personal test ploy with these initial inquiries.

"We'll talk soon," I say into the cordless phone. I release the hold on the other. "Sweetheart, I'm back. Thank you for holding. It's active around here today . . . So, how's your band holding up after eight weeks on the road?"

"We finished setting up. I look forward to seeing you," she says demurely.

"Of course, I will be coming to hear you sing tonight."

"Promise?"

"Mmmm . . . Yes, I promise baby, I'll be there." With my free hand I pull open my desk drawer. "I'm really looking forward to seeing you tonight." With one hand, I find a ring box and flip it open with my thumb to reveal a sparkling diamond ring. I flip it shut quickly and reclose the desk drawer. "But right now, I've got New York's Bart Levy on that sofa across from my desk. So, I've got to go now . . . Kisses to you, baby. Bye-bye."

Bart steps up to roam over the office walls. He closely examines the autographs, inscriptions on each of the aging and hanging show posters, plaques, banners, framed comic photos and caricatures of famous comics. He even stretches his neck to read the ceiling's plastered show bills from various shows of years past. The common banner headlining always reads THE ROUTE SIXTY-SIX COMEDY CLUB ROAD COMPANY Proudly Presents . . .

Finishing the phone call, I stretch my ears from being phone flattened. "I've got to get one of those phone headsets.

"Hey, Bart, good to see ya, man. How's life as a Conestoga comic been treating ya?"

I stand up to shake his hand.

"I've got to say something about your gigs. Greco . . ." he says. "They may be a string of one-nighters and countless hours apart, scattered throughout the Southwest, but they sure are fun," he shakes my hand. "I'm looking forward to that gig at Cannon Air Force Base tomorrow. Last time I was there, those air men treated me like a king." He sits back down, "Even though it's located in the middle of Nowhereville."

"Don't forget that nice paycheck and the strong stage time in front of large comedy-hungry audience," I insist.

Bart nods in agreement while placing a sealed white envelope on my desk. "That should take care of your commissions for this week from all of the comics."

Opening it with a letter opener, I count ten one-hundred-dollar bills. "Your Roswell gig for this UFO fifty-year celebration will get you some national TV exposure." I tell him. "There's plenty of media down there now, I understand."

"Never hurts, does it?"

"Then take Interstate Ten through southern New Mexico and into your Arizona run. Phoenix then Tucson will get you to San Diego for the weekend then up into Los Angeles for the following week. I've got you well secured."

Bart nods. "Hey, did you know that you have a big rep back in New York as the comedy godfather of the Southwest? Did you know that?" he asked in his Brooklyn accent.

I smile, "That is humbling to learn." The phone rings again.

Bart says, "Go ahead, I've got to use your john anyway." He steps out of the office as I pick up the cordless phone.

"Hello. Route Sixty-Six Comedy Club Road Company, Ronn speaking."

"Okay, Ronn?" says the female voice through the phone. "This is Johnney, Alpine's girlfriend."

I hesitate. My gut tells me this isn't good news.

"Oh yes." She is very familiar to me. She's been Alpine's salvation in turning that guy around. "How are you gal?"

"Well sir, I have some bad news. Bob has died."

The news sets me back. I am actually speechless.

"We knew he was sick . . . but . . ."

"His hard living finally caught up with him . . ."

I now can detect her tears. I credit Johnney for turning Alpine around. He centered more on the improvement of his lifestyle. He lived this long because of Johnney, is what I know.

"Well what are your plans? I mean to say, how can I help you?" Suddenly I am distracted as Bart Levy reenters. I try to refocus, but I can't. "Listen Johnney, are you at home?"

"Yes, I have so many arrangements to make . . ."

"I am coming over now to see you. Talk to you shortly okay?"

Suddenly I swivel around in my chair to see the Duke City Comedy Club All Stars group photo pinned to my office wall. The Chinatown banner is hanging over our heads. One of the standing comics behind me as I kneel is Alpine Bob.

A knot grows in my gut. "I remember that photo from years ago." I spin around in my desk as Bart Levy sits. "Those guys were my comics." Levy seems to detect a crackling emotion in my voice. I point to Alpine. "That sonofabitch, that sonofabitch." All I can do is shake my head.

I stand up straight.

'Alpine is dead?' is all I can think to myself. But still, I feel compelled to keep it to myself.

Bart Levy also stands. "Oh, yeah, now that I feel much better, I'm ready to tackle the drive ahead of me," he buckles his belt. I remain silent. "If I take off now, I should make Roswell by dark."

The phone rings showing the caller ID. "It's area code 213. That's L.A. Oh, hell. I'll call them back."

I always send my male comics back onto the road with a hearty handshake. If they were female, I'd hug them. So, I raise both arms with open palms of over my head into high fives. Bart Levy high fives me in return by slapping both open palms into mine. He then opens his palms at his waist level for me to slap them down in return. I do.

The phone rings again and is again ignored.

"Go ahead, answer it. I'll call ya when I get there."

After shaking his hand once again, I watch New Yorker Bart Levy close the screen door behind himself.

There is now an unexpected matter to take care of. I find myself studying the eight by ten inch black and white photograph of my old Duke City Comedy Club All Stars. The eight comics in all, captures my fixation. Knowing that they have all scattered into the wind in the ten plus years since, I smile at the floppy tam hat cocked over Alpine's head.

Chapter Thirty-Nine

Five years later

Wide eyed and eager faces look up to me as I stand in front of them in a college classroom. The black vinyl stage backdrop drapes from the ceiling to the floor and ten feet side to side behind me. Route Sixty-Six Comedy Club in gold leaf lettering is emblazoned on it.

Twenty aspiring student humorists sit in front of me, listening intently to every word I say. Three quarters are female. With pen or pencil in hand, they take notes.

"So, ladies and gentlemen, you paid forty-five dollars to attend this series of classes to see what the business behind the comedy club scene really is and to see if the comedy biz could really be for you. The good news is there is always a place for 99 percent of people who live and breathe the art of the laugh." I study their faces. "There is always a niche for the individual. Whether it is as a comic, producer . . ." I point to myself, "or as a manager, agent, booker, or publicist or for one or two of you someday, as club owner." I notice two of the cocky young guys in the back are posturing.

For the last several years I've been proud to stand on this spot conveying knowledge I've personally developed over my fifteen years in the biz. It's given me great satisfaction. The thought that what I've wrought over the last decade and a half has value to others always amazes me. Judging by some of the facial expressions from the older students, none knew what a comedy club was when I started the Duke City Comedy all those years ago. And to the younger ones, the comedy club has always been there.

"So, folks, there is no better place to start than at the beginning, which was long before any of us were born. I am talking about where today's modern comedy club business has its roots." I direct a question to a mature student. "Where did standing in front of strangers to tell jokes all start?"

The class focuses on my every word. "IT IS TRUTH, LADIES AND GENTLEMEN, THAT BY KNOWING YOUR HISTORY, YOU ARE BETTER POSITIONED TO PICK UP ITS POSITIVE LESSONS AND AVOID THE MISTAKES AND THEREBY BETTER GUIDE YOUR FUTURE. AND, IN THIS CASE, YOUR COMEDY CAREER."

All the faces tune in acutely. These are the facts I personally believe and have learned by doing. So, I continue, "It is believed in the English speaking world that the first comedians were the funky dressed court jesters. But they only had to make one person laugh and that was the king." I talk to another interested face, "If this king laughed, it was likely everybody else laughed." I face another student, "But for our purposes, we want to make everybody laugh. We know that clowns with the baggy pants or funny costumes, often prop oriented, mostly male individuals started making themselves known shortly after the American Civil War," I smile at a female student, "Credit goes to the circus king, P.T. Barnum, for originating the structured presentation of a variety show. He coined the name Vaudeville about this time. These shows were presented at Barnum's New York Museum auditorium and consisted of a variety of performing individuals."

Now standing center in front of the class, "These performers were initially used as sideshow diversions for his museum attractions, much like casinos do today to draw in gamblers."

A hand pops up in the rear of the room. She asks, "Did the migration west help?"

From front and center, I nod my head. "To gain more work back then, performers would spread to Conestoga wagon medicine shows. These shows were seldom in one place very long. And, as some of the 19th century saloons started presenting more and more entertainment, one comic was always included to MC or cover the gap between acts. This comedian always had the lowest billing, if they had billing at all. They were just there to fill the time between strippers, dancers, singers and even animal acts! Then around the late 1880's, known saloons and theaters back east that hired live entertainment, started linking up and were better able to afford traveling talents."

I take direct aim with my delivery to each and every face in this classroom. My intent is to find facial expressions of interest and/or understanding from each as a sign that I'm reaching them. In the second row sits a gray-haired, smiling grandmotherly type, with a walking cane on the floor beside her. Her bubbly personality radiates enthusiasm that reaches up to me. So, I direct toward her. "So, Jane, these venues that were short distances from each other developed into a circuit. And as this further circuit developed and strengthened, the business would be called Vaudeville.

Around the turn of the century, a risqué off shoot of the business developed into what was called Burlesque. It became a standard up and through the early sixties, for comics to play strip tease or topless joints. Because of this perceived relationship, comics and strippers became synonymous up and through that generation. Because many did become couples in real life. One example would be New York comic headliner Lenny Bruce and his lady."

My focus is directed toward the prim and proper, well-manicured, sophisticated lady sitting on the other side of the room, "And so, Doctor Touchman, may I call you Gail?" She nods, so I continue. "As a psychiatrist, you know that humor has healing and medicinal affects." Ronn sees her nod. "You may be interested to note that to this day, there are still those who fail to give the respect due. For instance, in the theatrical field itself, if you can imagine, there are some, the ones with their noses in the air, who consider the comic to be the black sheep of the theatrical family."

Without missing a beat, I turn toward the chubby fifteen-year-old boy politely listening with wide eyes behind big glasses sitting in the front row. "It wasn't until the late seventies and the early eighties that the comedy club began to come into its own. It quickly became the theater of stand-up comedy. This has permitted the image of the stand-up comic to positively develop which led to more respect for what it takes to perform the art. And is why you are here tonight."

This time I focus my direction toward the short hair, tie wearing, computer executive sitting next to his fellow comic student and chubby son, "So, Randy, one of the last institutions that grant the stand-up comic respect is, strangely enough, the theatrical acting community themselves! The black sheep of the theater family still prevails. They begrudgingly accept the fact that comics are legitimately part and parcel of the theatrical business, too. So, if you ever confront a snob, just tell them it only takes one comic to entertain that same size of an audience that it takes two to four actors to do."

I am happy to get a laugh from my class. "Plus, comics can become actors easier than actors can become comics. On top of that, comics are their own writers. Seldom do you find an actor writing his own play. Hold your head up high when you say that you are a stand-up comic," I state with pride. "Now to some specifics on starting your comic career. Any questions so far?"

Hands shoot up. A tall, lanky, t-shirt wearing Generation Xer with blond spiked hair and a ring piercing his left ear asks, "How long can we perform for next week's class?"

"Be easy on yourself. Start with two or three jokes."

"Three jokes! Jeez, I can go on for hours!" the kid answers.

How many times have I heard that response, I think.

"Listen. When you get onto that live stand-up comedy stage with hot and bright stage lights directly in your face, know that every eye in the place is on YOU! And if you still think that you can go on for hours, you'll go to the head of this class. Till then, be easy on yourself."

"Are there that many female comics working the comedy clubs?" wonders a middle aged, well dressed housewife type.

"Oh yes. Right now, lady comics are hot. The truly talented ladies are working steady. As a matter of fact, I like to present lady comics as often as I can afford them." I pick up a sense of approval from that student.

"This nightclub that we're performing at next week, will the audience have to pay to get in?" a clean-cut fellow in the back of this student gang shouts out.

"Are you ready to sell your routines? You need stage time with an audience more than you need to make money right now. Just invite your friends because you will want all the friendly laughter you can get, you'll see."

"How soon will it take for us to get paid doing this?" asks a hard-looking female in boots and cowgirl hat.

"It all depends when you get a commercial-length act developed. Build your emceeing talents with the goal of building toward your Opener's fifteen-minute act. Then build to the features slot of thirty minutes. The headliner has to do forty-five to sixty minutes. Each slot gets enumerated accordingly."

I'm relieved that there are so many interested questions from this class. It tells me that I've gotten through to them.

Chapter Forty

The University of New Mexico nighttime campus is as busy as it is under daylight as I walk to my car parked acres away from the classroom. And I am anxious to get home where a couple of special people are waiting for me.

The terra-cotta architecture of the surrounding campus buildings cut a silhouette against the Daylight Savings Time sky as the sun sinks over the west horizon. Adjacent campus sections of older buildings utilize pueblo architecture. Their exterior kiva beams are protruding. The combined affect is truly New Mexican ambiance.

With my briefcase in one hand, I turn my cell phone back on with the other. I press various numbers and codes to retrieve my voice messages. Quickly pacing my steps over the campus, I skip through many of them. I'll answer later when I can concentrate. I place the phone back into my breast pocket. After a few more steps, the cell phone chimes in with the Beethoven's Fifth. As I maintain my steady pace toward a distant parked car, I answer it. "Hello, Route Sixty-Six Comedy Club. Ronn Greco here!"

"Am I lucky enough to finally track down that Godfather of Comedy out there?" comes an exuberant male voice.

I detect a slight male New York accent without yet recognizing the caller. "Yes, sir. Ronn Greco here," maintaining my pace. The cell phone reception is raspy.

"I had to give you a call. You'd be pissed at me if I didn't." the voice says as he expects me to recognize the voice.

Stalling for time, I go along with the moment. "It probably would not have been the first time either, right?" trying to recognize this, one of the countless voices that I've spoken to today.

"How in the hell are you, big guy? Life out here in Hollywood is funky and jaded as all get out. But I had to call you to tell ya!" came the excited voice out of the little box in my hand.

Hollywood with a slight New York accent, it could only be one guy. "I haven't heard from you in months, bud! How's the comedy and acting career of Bart Levy coming?" My pace continues toward a distant parked automobile.

"I did it! I finally made it Ronn! That's why I wanted to get hold of you as soon as possible. I'm on the Tonight Show tonight! We've finished taping an hour ago. You gotta tune in." Legitimate excitement comes from Bart Levy. "I was advised not to contact anyone till afterward. Just in case I was cut at the last minute. Which has been known to happen."

I stop in my tracks at the great news.

"That's fantastic! Congratulations you S.O.B. That's great! How did your performance go? Did you get a chance to sit next to Leno?"

"Well, tune in tonight and see for yourself. But that's not all, man! Are you sitting down?"

I'm standing alone in the middle of the large courtyard style campus. "In that case, give me a moment, I'll find a nice seat." I place it around the wishing pool of a water fountain.

"I've got the lead in a new sitcom pilot! What do you think of them apples?" Bart Levy practically shouts.

Ronn responds by proudly saying, "And I can sincerely say, I knew you when . . ."

Chapter Forty-One

Each of the multiple hanging lights focus on their specific area of the theatrical stage setting. The executive office set is designed to easily identify as it shows a window revealing the Washington Monument in the far background. Each light lamp radiates encompassing warmth throughout the Hollywood Fox television studio. Silence captures the hundreds of people in the audience gallery behind a three-camera setup. All in the room focus on the two actors, male and female, on the set.

So, this is how it's done, I think. A Hollywood television sitcom pilot taping is unique. I feel privileged to be the guest of one of the two actors now on the stage. The enjoyment includes viewing the action from the front row of the surrounding live audience. Sitting in the center chair with GUEST written on the back of it, I'm extra careful to be silent. The cherry red light on the center camera on the floor level below me suddenly flashes on. A laughter prompter sign overhead flashes on.

I've never seen the female actor before. But when one of my old comics calls me from Hollywood, I naturally have to tease him. Not expecting to, but jokingly, I ask to be invited to the taping. And I was!

I located a couple gigs here in Southern California to help pay the way. Tonight and tomorrow's shows are in smoggy San Bernardino, California at the ROCKET THEATER, a former topless bar.

But today, I'm in Hollywood, California. I'm on the 20th Century Fox movie lot. Stage B 2. We're watching the pilot taping of what I hope will eventually be a long running sitcom. Why? Because it's being acted in by one of my former comics, since, turned friend.

It's about the political life and times of a married couple in Washington D.C. She's an advisor for a Republican Congressman and Bart Levy plays a lobbyist with Democratic leaning.

I sit here remembering when I hired him. When he first worked his way cross country for me from New York to Flagstaff to Hollywood all those years ago. The acting and writing bug was his goal even then. Like many, many comic writer/actors before him, stand-up comedy has been his vehicle. He's since given up touring to dedicate more time to the craft of getting his scripts produced and getting acting jobs. With this pilot, Bart Levy has double gold as writer/actor.

I sit and study the camera angles and how the actors walk through their blocking. The center camera's red light snaps on while another flashes off with a third camera taking its eventual rotation. Quickly turning and glancing around to the rear of the studio, I see the tech booth up and above the audience gallery. Turning back to the action, I see heat waves emit from the lights that loom over the set. Why the actors aren't sweating is amazing. It has to be very hot under those things.

Script in hand, the female floor director stands between two of the three cameras. Her sudden obvious grimacing indicates that the actress apparently has flubbed one of her lines. The audience nevertheless laughs despite the laugh prompter overhead not going on. Before taping started today, Bart told me that later in post-production the laugh tracks will be added to augment audience laughter. This floor director snaps the script book shut to relax as the audience gives her unexpected moment of hilarity.

As Bart Levy embraces then kisses his lovely female lead, the applause sign flashes, and the audience obliges. The floor director silently mouths a five count to her crew along with counting down the fingers on her right hand before the stage lights go dark. A moment passes before the much cooler house lights snap back on. Applause begins to fill the studio. The five-member cast skips out from behind the set's wings to a spot lit area at stage center. All link hands and take a bow in unison. Audience applause peaks for a minute or so. Then the stage again goes dark as silhouette actors disappear into the stage wings. My enthusiasm is strong as I stand and applaud.

From behind the rear of the stage and before it has cooled down, a waiting crew of stagehands move out of the wood work. They coil up camera cables, others move out stage furniture. Some pull apart stage backdrops and dressings. The panel window with the capitol building painted on it is struck and carried off sideways by one stagehand. Only then does a lone individual emerge from behind one of the remaining stage flats.

Still in costume, a suit jacket with tie removed to reveal an open collar and rolled up sleeves, Bart Levy happily approaches me.

"Congratulations, Bart. Good show!" I shake my old comic's hand. "You are a topnotch comedy actor too!" I add.

"I was backstage practically biting my fingernails off. I appreciate the feedback," he confesses.

"I guess it goes with the territory when you are one of Hollywood's top, up and coming comedy sitcom actors," I slap Bart's shoulder. "This looks like network sitcom material to me. They'll buy it. Congratulations!"

Key studio work light fixtures turn on.

Bart smiles suddenly. "Remember when you first booked me years ago and offered me what would be our very first mutual congratulations!"

My mind is jerked back into time.

"Don't you remember Las Cruces?" he continues. "At the Coyote Comedy Club? We were at some country and western nightclub after the show and closed it down. We collected a gang that night that gathered outside afterward. At the same moment you took to offer us congratulations on the night, some well lubricated gal from our gang cornered us, then stuck her partially amputated arm in my face."

My memory snaps into place and I grin. "Yeah, and you immediately started singing into it like it was your stage microphone!"

"Hey, she played along too! Those people, our gang, laughed their guts out. Didn't they? Didn't they?"

At that moment we laugh together, and I glance at my watch. I have to hustle to get to my gig in San Bernardino, a couple of hours away. And I still have to get back to the hotel to shower and change.

"We're having a cast party tomorrow night at the Seaside Bar 'N Grill in Santa Monica. Why don't you come," says Bart.

"The plan is to fly home tomorrow. But let me make some phone calls and rearrangements. Of course, I'm gonna be there! I'm not known as the type to turn down an invitation to one of those famous Hollywood parties!"

Chapter Forty-Two

After spending seemingly all the next day waiting at John Wayne Airport, it's a pleasure for my desert loving eyes to finally gander over the bluish gray of the Pacific Ocean. This comedy club business has finally got me as far west as I can get while the sun is about to set. The soft waves roll over my bare feet.

I am thinking about the sign I just read. Entering this Santa Monica Pier, a wooden placard read, 'You Are Now at The End of America's Mother Road, ROUTE SIXTY-SIX.'

This highlights crazy thoughts that have been passing through my forty-eight-year-old mind lately. Am I too old for this biz?

I choose not to believe it. So, I make a pledge of sorts. Someday, someday I will take my road show to a point as far as I can and still speak English. Of course, they'd have to like Americans.

Straining my vision far over the Pacific waves, I know that Route Sixty-Six will not end in Hawaii either. A light bulb flashes on over my head as a new idea captures me. Ocean waves roll in deep enough to cover my ankles. The golden orange sun crest now barely peeks above the horizon.

The thought of being Down Under in Sydney, Australia slams into my brain. Smiles, giggles and laughs Down Under! I like the idea. Take the Route 66 farther than it has ever gone. Suddenly and unexpectedly, a sweet sound breaks my concentration.

"Daddy, Daddy, Mommy wants you," my little girl shouts with her arms stretched out wide. I catch Nicole in my arms, bringing with her the sand all over her little feet and hands. She kisses my cheek.

"Daddy, Mommy wants something to eat. I am hungry, too! Can we get a hambuger with mustar? Huh, Daddy?"

"Your wish is my command, baby. Let's go eat." Putting Nicole back onto the sand, I take her hand and brush the sand off my collar. Nancy walks up the beach toward us in her sundress. Enhanced by light from the ruby red sunset, my wife's crimson colored hair seems fiery. She slips her arm around my waist. I enjoy this opportunity of having them both together. "Did I ever tell you ladies that I love you very much?"

I put my arm around Nancy's waist. I seldom think about it, but she's grown a little hippier since the baby, and I've grown thicker around the middle. After holding the little hand of my daughter, life is great! And now I know what the future has in store for us.

Trailing behind, "Daddy I am tired."

So, I pick her up and place her around my head onto my shoulders as we walk down the sands.

With the sun sinking over the horizon, I hear the original song that I've enjoyed in many renditions over the years coincidently coming from a far off building. It's Nat King Cole's version, ". . . when making that California trip, get your kicks on the Route Sixty-Six . . ."

Epilogue

What has happened to some of the individuals you have just finished reading about? Glad you asked . . .

ROBIN CEE has become a mainstay in various world USO tours as the opening act for many of the top national celebrity comic performers. Her resume already includes a list of America's AAA comedy clubs, three times over. But she herself admits, the foreign country that has experienced her 6'1" footprints the most is Japan. "Because they all look up to me!"

WILLIAM (Call 'im Weely) CORDOVA has retired his stage persona. Also contented to have put in his years as a printer from the local newspaper, he's retired and now lives off his 401K. He and IRENE have bought a horse farm and now live off the soil. He says there is no more traveling throughout the nation's various comedy club circuits for him. "My lowrider don't ride there no more," he says. They are happy to frolic with their 12 grand kids.

As a matter of fact, his inspiration is now onto his daughter whose solidifying her initial fifteen minutes. If that's not all, his daughter's daughter is polishing her initial few minutes. So soon expect to see the only father, daughter, granddaughter act in the history of comedy on Planet Earth.

FRANK CROSBY (Call 'im Mr. Terrific!) never disclosed his age before he passed on. But it was roughly calculated during his Charity Celebrity Roast that was held shortly before his passing, it was guesstimated to be Eighty-Three Years. His best pal from his years in their mutual auto racetrack days decades earlier invited all his friends. Mayors, New Mexican Governors, auto racers (including two Indy 500 winners), country singers, bankers, media sports broadcasters, and Frank's favorite local comic, Weely Cordova and me. Frank's 15-member Big Band played their swing tunes to accompany the three-course dinner and big dance. At the end of the night, when time came for Frank to give his speech, all he could say to the smiling faces sitting in front of him was, "T-E-R-R-I-F-I-C!" He was still producing Big Band Dances to the end. He said he was not amazed that it's still popular with the young kids who love swing music. He was often a guest speaker at Ronn's comedy class. He also ran for mayor, again. His billboards read VOTE FOR ME, AND VOTE OFTEN. He says, "I don't need nor do I want a paycheck. I'll work for the graft."

After his passing, I read his book again. And it was very, very easy to see why he named his memoir, THEY CALL ME MR. TERRIFFIC !!

ANNI DANGER became a much in demand lady for USO tours at American military bases in Europe. Soon enough, the Cruise Ship circuits became her 50 weeks a year mainstay. Especially on ships that steam into the Bahamas. She's rented out her new Salt Lake City home but kept a portion of it available when she goes home between excursions. Along the way, her New York agent has been able to get her an occasional national TV appearance. She's even had her One Woman off-off-Broadway show, with a live orchestra yet!

So, professionally, life is great. All this while her Northern Hemisphere searches found that one perfect man. What is not funny is that she has not done a performance since he slid that ring on her finger.

HARRY JEW the New Chinatown Restaurant restaurateur, has passed on. He didn't realize it at the time of course, but his Route 66 egg roll eatery would be listed in the national comedy trades as the only Chinese restaurant with a comedy club in the entire country! The home of topnotch Mandarin eats would host the birth to the southwestern comedy club industry.

DAVE LEFKOWITZ still lives off the Pacific Ocean in Southern California. Giving up performing comedy was not difficult when he became a successful screenwriter. With several screenplays sold to his credit, he still spends part of his day rollerblading up and down the bike paths of Venice Beach.

BART LEVY still occasionally performs Ronn's comedy club circuits when he can break away from Hollywood. He has built and developed a strong character-actor career with five TV sitcom appearances to his credit. He flies now when he goes home to New York, but he still teases Ronn that someday he'll drive across country again so he can stop in Albuquerque at Ronn's office just to take a whiz.

PAUL LOTT worked hard to become a Duke City Comedy All Star, but his previous brain injury never allowed him to fully recover his previous professional magic performing abilities. One Halloween night, during the New Chinatown Restaurant days, he threw a costume party at a local coffee house. Of course, he headlined his party's show, and some of the DCCC All Stars opened for him. Part of their stage assignment was to carry onto the stage a makeshift coffin that he popped out of dressed like a vampire. Paul went on to perform the best show in people's memory that evening. But later that night he stuck his head into a gas oven. Everyone thought that he was on the mend and slowly but surely making a comeback. But instead, he had thrown his own wake.

BILLY McCARTHY, as of this writing, and as if anyone cares, sits in the Arizona State Penitentiary for groping and having his way with a 12-year-old girl in a swimming pool. When he gets out, there is one thing for sure. Talented comics have been known to make professional comebacks after spending time in the slammer for drug convictions, murders, arson, and counterfeiting and so on. But in his case, unless he changes his name and goes where they don't know him, no one will have anything to do with him. Most people already deny ever knowing him, including me.

JAKE PEIRSON has gone on to be a successful ventriloquist, performing all of the national comedy club circuits and is a favorite on the cruise ship circuit. Several years ago, after ten years of working for Ronn, he quit. The competition told him not to work for the opposing comedy operation. They waved more money in his face. I am still sensitive to the snub. So, when the competitor's limited opportunities dried up, Jake was forced to leave town. Being a strong talent, he landed on his feet by moving to Dallas where he opened and now runs his own comedy club.

BILL MICHEALS, decades later after leaving the U. S. Marines, as a captain, he went on to pursue a comedy career in New York. In no time his star rose. He had his own comedy TV show on the national comedy cable channel COMEDY CENTRAL, which then led to his own successful HBO comedy Special. In his comedy rise to the top, he tells everyone how he got his start in a Chinese restaurant, in a small town called Albuquerque. He married a Victoria Secrets' model and now raises their two daughters in Bridgeport, Conn. While he produces comedy TV specials, he occasionally plays road dates. But he is quoted as saying that he must keep the gigs close and around the northeast due to wanting to stay close to the family. His only regret he states is that he admits his addiction to red and green chile.

SILVER VEGA is still doing her brand of comedy and is still single. She also receives gratification from her coast-to-coast notoriety and financial success in her jewelry manufacturing endeavors. Her southwestern designs have been purchased by movie stars, a United States first lady and many others of influence. She briefly succumbed to the ultimatum. "Perform for the competing comedy club or perform for Greco." She chose them, but quickly found that Ronn had more gigs and was forgiving, so she returned to him. About this time, a protest took place in Santa Fe, New Mexico. Catholic groups were in an uproar about a new painting in a public gallery that depicted the Mary of Guadalupe in a bikini. In defense of the artist, Silver came to show her support in a similar bikini. And because she still looks fine, she started performing her comedy act in it. At least until the shock wore off. All this proves is that yes, you can still find an endless supply of Smiles, Giggles and Laughs while you GET YOUR KICKS ON RT 66.

About the Author

Ronn Perea's previous novels were created around his years in theatrical stage production with his propensity for Tango dancing and world traveling adventures. He enjoys taking his fans where they never historically imagined going before. He always enjoys asking, "Did you know that this and that happened…?" Then he usually responds to the usual wide-eyed expectancy of, "Tell me more . . .." He always aims to please.

**A LIFE SHAPING RELATIONSHIP WILL GROW BETWEEN
TWO HIGH SCHOOL GIRLS ELSIE AND ELSA...**

During the mid-20th century, many historical events occurred in the American Southwest that shaped the lives of many families. This story brings to light those events and the people that changed the course of history...

For more information
visit: www.SpeakingVolumes.us

Made in the USA
Middletown, DE
24 January 2023

22685288R00128